SPELL OF THE PELICANS

SPELL OF THE PELICANS

J.L. COOPER

Carmichael, CA / 2018

Foreword

James Cooper, my father, passed away before he could write this foreword. He had been terminally ill for the entirety of his published writing career, but wrote and created tirelessly. It was his wish for his poems and stories to survive him, to leave us with great, enduring beauty in the wake of such pain.

Though this book is not about him, strictly speaking, there is so much of him in it. The story draws inspiration from his experiences: as a clinical psychologist, son, father, husband, aquatic adventurer and lifeguard, seeker of ancient wisdom, and keen student of the human condition. But beyond his experiences, my father's qualities and the essence of who he was flows through his writing. He appears to me as a river, winding and playful, bubbling with a whimsical curiosity, a tributary feeding into a deep and patient lagoon that feeds into the ocean, a place to which he had great love and connection. From somewhere beneath the surface of what we know, secrets, insights, mysteries and truths drift elegantly to the surface, bringing forth hidden meaning and an inquisitive smile.

One of the last things my father said to me before he died was this: "Always remember, I am with you in so many ways." This book is one of those ways. May you know and appreciate him more through his stories and poems. For truly, in the simple joy of perfectly buttered popcorn, in the wonder of fireworks blooming overhead, as well as in life's most enduring, transcendent truths: Always remember, he is with us, in so many ways, now and forever.

Cameron Cooper
October 14, 2018

Disclaimer

Names and characters are the product of the author's imagination and are used fictitiously to represent themes of the human condition. Any resemblance to actual persons in the clinical practice of the author, living or dead, is coincidental.

Orange County Beaches

Distances on map are approximate

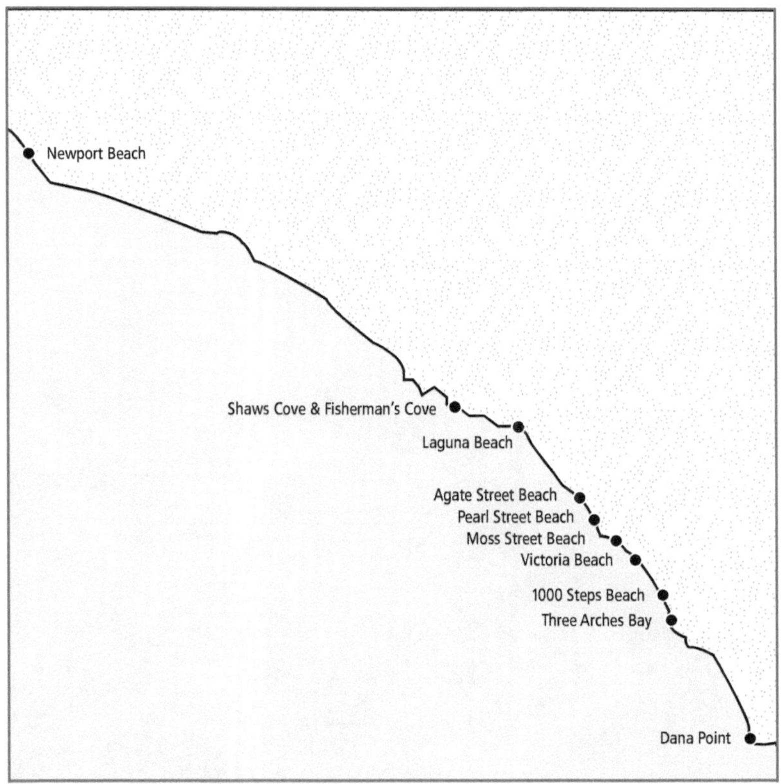

Chapter One

A FEAST OF GRAYS

Lean forward, cup your eyes, look to the misty sea. Six brown pelicans form a perfect line, a hundred yards offshore, wings just inches above the glassy Pacific. You can freeze the image at Laguna Beach, tuck it away to visit at will. If you close your eyes and look again, other canvases appear. A dozen gulls are quarreling downwind, and out to sea, two bottlenose dolphins circle each other, languid, at play, without a destination. The scene is a feast of grays. Even the urgent gulls seem more distant than they are, and the barking seals offshore are muted by the rule of fog. A spell has been cast on humans, diminishing their importance. Serene waves crumble rather than break on the crescent beach, without making a sound. They kiss the shore again and again, receding with equal grace.

To the man transfixed at the edge of water, the ocean is a veiled woman coming to be with him. She lifts her veil halfway, pauses in the certainty of knowing him, kisses his cheek, his brow, finally his lips, then backs away in mist, leaving him to wonder why she offers such scented intimate ways yet hides the nature of her eyes. He can't understand his fortune and wonders if he invented her or if she's a gift from the ceaseless waves. Either way, the ocean rests today. Sand turns thoughts to grains and won't release a meaning. Tempests are deferred to a Mexican storm and the man who can't locate the source of his reverie finds love from an earlier century. Locked in the cell phone in his pocket is the music of Arcangelo Corelli, master of the Concerti Grossi.

He places the ear buds in gently, first the left, and fills his lungs with fresh salt air. After all, Hatley Pierce is a lefty, and presses the *play* button with a private smile, opening to the music while closing his mind to the last six months of rough going in his psychotherapy practice, a hundred miles inland, five hundred miles up north in Sacramento. At least he's within walking distance to the American River, flowing westward through the great central valley of California. It's beautiful along the banks, a riparian paradise, but here at the edge of the continent, the flow comes down to this; all water is kindred but the ocean has no peer.

He'd planned for a morning swim, bracing for the jolt of immersion. Coffee first, then a walk along the boardwalk, taking long slow strides and even longer breaths. The beaches of childhood were calling. Other matters too; the impossible one. It was no use trying to push it away. He needed to see an old friend and mentor. Need has a way of churning, like the backside of a wave about to suck you in. You know that dread surrender, right when you thought you'd dived safely through its belly. There you are in the washing machine, humbled, curled up, smashed to the ocean floor, waiting until it's safe to come up for air.

The trouble with finding Dr. Benjamin Morissy was that he was dead. The outer world had mourned him, had written kindly of his contributions to psychoanalysis. Memories that Pierce had put to bed came rushing back in a flood. Pierce was the only person aware of another chapter, the only one burdened by the unthinkable nature of what Morissy had done five years ago; faked his own death during a depressive episode, when his clinical career was still going strong. A year ago, Pierce discovered that Morissy was still alive, living a second life with a mix of persistence and curiosity. He couldn't change his nature and couldn't tell his story to the world he left behind. Pierce looked for an angle to justify an intrusion, realizing how everything comes around in another form, in a winged or tumbling way, like his close call just that morning on the Santa Ana freeway. He saw a car flip over and barely missed being part of a pile-up. Later, he heard on the radio nobody died in the crash, but he filed the moment as a warning. What to make of witnessing? Frailty had paid him another visit and he resolved to look for Morissy even if it brought him trouble. The man owed him, after all. Carrying such a secret is a conundrum. Pierce needed to find his lost mentor, the one person who always helped him with complications, even though Morissy was the biggest complication of all.

But Corelli wasn't finished with Pierce. If the shifting winds were Corelli's instruments, the musical score hailed from the fine-grained sand until the notes became sheets of silk drifting across the boardwalk. An unseen concertmaster used his violin to summon the past and future without announcing the merits of either. The recording was so rich, it brought the soul of Arcangelo, returning from his tomb to conduct the sea and air, while Pierce's thirty-five years of being a psychotherapist came and vanished in the pause between the Concerto No. 3 in C minor and the No. 4 in D major. He inserted all of his life into the pause; it gets easier with the years.

Surrender to Corelli was the goal, while the white mist yielded to the sun, and long tones merged in grand and patient textures with flurries of eighth and sixteenth notes. The minor keys were as welcome as the major ones—each registered a sideways glance to the pause between winter and the June gloom to come. In the silence between pieces, Pierce wondered who had brought this serious tone, this mirror's edge, to the stunning April morning? The only certainty in his mind was the day belonged to Corelli.

Chapter 2

SHAPES THAT DISAPPEAR

A private smile is the best smile, and Pierce found one to suit the fact that nobody in the psychoanalytic community suspected Dr. Benjamin Morissy faked his own death. He was one of the greats, stellar in thought, challenging orthodoxy while weaving his ideas into unfinished tapestries, never implying a summary. A fully stocked sailboat with a broken rudder had been found in Lake Michigan the morning after a day of thunderstorms. The body was never discovered, only a life vest that was clasped and possibly had come off. Lake Michigan could be that way. Nobody witnessed the lone sailboat on the horizon that evening, with a storm bearing down from the northeast, but a few people saw him launch in seemingly good spirits, whistling an Irish tune. It was not the demeanor of a man who appeared to be sad. If the water could tell, it would say he took fins for the long swim to shore after dark, two miles in choppy water, using a wetsuit and a lighted waterproof compass, headed for a deserted campground and a beat-up car with no registration.

All of it was carefully planned: plenty of cash, a plane ticket to Argentina for plastic surgery, and a new identity he'd been working on secretly. He was already fluent in Spanish, and would re-invent himself as Javier, live a quiet life in San Miguel de Allende, Mexico, pretending to be a retiree from the rat race up north. He got a new passport on the black market, a new Social Security card, just like spies in movies. Those parts were surprisingly easy. Money wasn't an issue. He fancied himself as amiable, a retired carpenter, writing stories, reading history, trying his hand at painting, partial to the ladies. The plan worked beautifully the first few years, not so much the aftermath. As Javier, he had to make himself over and over, expand the template, edit his own fiction, until he started leaking around the edges, returning to his sadness.

How could he do it? thought Pierce. How could he live with the images of people grieving him, especially those in the middle of therapy? *Why did he do it?* When colleagues would have supported him no matter the severity of his depression, even those who envied him. Depression is often treatable, he reminded himself, at least partially. A student of his once said that horrible things make sense when the mind stays dark for too long, and of course she was right. A few of Morissy's conservative colleagues resented him for his gall to suggest that therapists are at least as confusing to their patients as the other way around. He loved asking a particular question;

"Why should we presume to bring about changes in others that we can't make in ourselves? It's not easy to accept how much we're in love with our beliefs and models while sometimes being closed to what our patients are trying to say to us." For all the controversy surrounding him, nobody wished him gone.

Standing in the dry sand, Pierce recalled how their colleagues were shocked with the news of Morissy's death, but some observed he was becoming withdrawn and had gone into a tailspin that year. He never elaborated on his internal world, just faded bit by bit from the outer one. A colleague recalled a comment from him during a supervision group he was leading.

"In a difficult moment, never blame the patient, then you have no other option but to look to yourself for something you don't really want to know. I used to accomplish that. Now I'm not so sure." He stumbled through what he was trying to say, which was unusual; then he tried revising the sentence, inverting his thoughts, but instead he stared at a lone paperclip on the floor for a terribly long minute. Some of the students had the impression of an old wound visiting.

Nobody had to look far. Morissy's wife, June, the rose of his life, had died of cancer the year before, after a savagely short illness. Morissy seemed weirdly dignified about it all. In the past, he'd shown more grief and anger about much smaller losses, but in that earthquake, there was only a hint of resignation, a sigh, something nobody really understood. He was unapproachable on the subject, even from friends.

Who could do anything but support him when he took up sailing? He sailed the upstate lakes of New York, the shallow lakes in Minnesota, all the while heading for larger bodies of water, where he'd sail out of sight of land on clear summer nights, then navigate home by the stars.

Pierce was one of the few who knew from the horse's mouth that Morissy's parents died in a car accident when he was seven, right when he imagined having superpowers. He had no siblings to help him carry the common memories.

"You know," Morissy said, supervising a case, "by the time I was twelve, I thought I could make up just about anything and live in my own inventions. I figured I owed it to myself to create a private world that could protect me when bad things happen. All I really knew was that I wasn't going to be defined as the poor kid who lost his parents. I had all these theories brewing. Beyond that, I had no idea what I was reacting to; adolescence was coming on, the world was rushing toward me." Pierce remembered the day they reconnected.

Chapter 3

DISCOVERY

It was exactly a year ago, on a similar trip when Pierce was visiting his favorite beaches. He took a drive inland to shop for antique bookends near the Orange Circle in the city of Orange and went to the liquor store on the corner to buy the racing form for the night's quarter horse races at Los Alamitos. It was his tradition. It's what his mother did before computers came along. On recent visits, whether he went out to the track or not, Pierce would buy the racing form, not flowers, and bring it to his mother's grave. He'd tear out the relevant pages, fold them, place them in the cup where flowers go, and ask if she had any advice—on the races that is. She had a system, numerology combined with her own arcane method of handicapping that produced unusual accuracy with exactas and trifectas. He tried to study it, to learn it, but the critical factors changed daily. She couldn't teach it anymore than you can teach a person to be who they are. He hoped she would figure the races from beyond and just tell him, give him a sign, since she dabbled in ESP, loved Houdini, slight of hand, and other occult matters. But on that day there was no call from beyond, unless it was she who sent him to the Orange Circle, to the man at a little popcorn stand who handed him a large bag of buttered popcorn.

The man held it the same way Dr. Morissy used to hold his coffee cup during all those Manhattan mornings in clinical supervision, thumb pointing slightly upward, tight-fisted, leaning a tiny bit forward, round shoulders, staring forward in a kind of eternal amusement. Pierce instantly recognized the hand and worked his way up to the eyes. How could this unlikely man remind him so vividly of his mentor? Plastic surgery could not disguise the novel in the eyes.

Benjamin Morissy was no less surprised than Pierce at the moment of recognition. With a mix of shock and shame, he changed the price of popcorn.

"Dr. Hatley Pierce, I presume. That'll cost you three dollars sir, plus I'll ask you to bring me a decent case and not hold back a single detail. I've changed my profession as you can see." Then he added, in a goofy embarrassed way, "I guess you've discovered I'm not dead. I've worried about this day. I've dreaded it. I should have stayed in Mexico, but I admit, it's a relief that it's you who found me."

They stood in the stunned aftermath of the moment. Pierce thought of punching him in the face for not being dead, and wanted to pummel him further for being glib. Neither could believe the other was standing toe-to-toe, but neither could deny the flood. The meeting was like a dream, oddly natural, but split off from the usual frames of time and place. Then, as surely as a squall on the horizon, confessions and apologies issued from the old man.

"I owe you an explanation. It will be pathetic, but it will be true."

"You sure as hell do owe me, I expect it to be pathetic. I can't believe it's you." He took two steps back and paused while cars circled around behind them. "By the way, I inherited a patient of yours when you fake-died. I'll need a bit of supervision, or would you prefer to explain it to her directly? She's been imagining you're still alive, by the way. I've been seeing her for four years. What the hell happened to you?"

"What could I possibly offer anyone now, even you, now that I've crossed that bridge?

"You won't be the judge. Shut up and let me think."

Thinking was not on the menu, and in it's place, questions kept tumbling. Waverly told him the details of his *Mexico Solution,* as he called it, along with the plastic surgery, fake name and ID's and the careful cover stories.

"Look," said Pierce, "I've always known you're clever, I'm asking about the reasons."

"I did a cowardly thing, hoping for a tidy exit. Boxed myself into a corner after my wife died. I couldn't work through my own depression after insisting my whole career that no grief is unreachable. I made my own death start to make sense. Hate me for it. I do. I was in therapy even, and you couldn't believe my acting job. Never mentioned my plan. Privately, I rationalized everything. I wanted to die, to follow my wife when I had prostate surgery. I even hoped my cancer was terminal; it would have been honorable. But you know the nature of dread. I saw my wife through every moment of her illness. In the end, she was ready to go and I was the one who couldn't let go. In the months after, a kind of trap door opened in me, and I cooked up a way to start over, to not have obligations. Patients had been telling me how vital I was in their lives, but I felt shame that I couldn't prevent the suffering of my wife. I left everyone, and for what? It was incredibly selfish. I wasn't counting on having to witness myself. Like you say, such the clever one. How's that for cheating death?"

Morissy stopped talking, and for a goodly while he couldn't meet the steely eyes in front of him. Eyes that wanted more. The silence made Morissy swell, if only to fill the void.

"There were side effects I didn't see coming, an expression I couldn't find in the new face, also the absurd contrast between the wish for a contemplative life in another culture and the way I really am. Soon, the ghastly dreams returned, the loss of weight, of appetite, the blunting of curiosity; familiar signs I was sliding into depression again. I'm tired. I've run out of fresh things to say about my past. The problem was that people always liked me and wanted me to tell stories. I'm not so good at lying as you might think. Anyway, it didn't sit well with me. Now that I'm a popcorn guy, nobody asks what I did before."

Pierce softened. "It must feel like a curse that you've always been stunningly good at listening."

"At least I get to have conversations and practice the art of watching. This new face still throws me off every time I look in a mirror." He didn't mention there was only one mirror in his home that he usually covered with a towel. "You were one of the very few who visited me in the hospital when I had my surgery. Know this; shame turns into a river and empties into the depths of the ocean. When I wanted to die, little signs kept appearing to me, lights burning out in my hallway, finding myself in tears in the back of cabs, asking to be driven to the Hudson River, where I'd walk and walk without making eye contact with anyone. Depression is cunning; don't underestimate the undercurrents. I'll ask the unfair thing, please don't let on I'm alive. I'm begging."

"No fiction is stranger than real life. I won't reveal this to your colleagues or anyone we know, maybe to the ocean, since the ocean is large enough to hold all that we are."

Chapter 4

PRECIPICE

Pierce couldn't believe what he was hearing. His throat was as parched as the crusty shore of the Salton Sea. The plea opened a door to a memory of one of Morissy's lectures when he was a young trainee, seeing the great thinker in front of a crowd thirty years ago. When lecturing, Morissy was famous for standing at the edge of a precipice of some kind, however small, or just implied. A piece of black tape on the floor would have to suffice when he didn't have a podium. He had a shining presence, always bringing himself to some kind of edge on purpose. Sometimes he'd stand with his feet just a few inches over the edge of the stage, and every five minutes or so, he'd look down at the edge, but never mention it.

Pierce invited himself to probe the image and try a rookie move; to tell Morissy he was fascinated by the precipice business. It was fun to play, even if it was folly or flat out wrong.

"When you come up to the edge like that, I wonder if there's a purpose. You must sense a collective concern in the audience, something meant to be both literal and symbolic."

What Pierce really wanted to say was that by looking down, then resuming his talk, Morissy seemed to be speaking to the maddening observation for which a logical solution never comes. Surely he knew some people were wondering, *why doesn't the man step back from the edge? What's his point? He could fall. Is this some phobia or ritual?* Sometimes, the gathering of psychotherapists offered a collective laugh, a nervous laugh. But Morissy never commented. His business with the precipice became something of a trademark. His black unpolished shoes persisted at the edge until the lecture was over, then he'd back away, always three steps, and walk sideways off the stage.

The backdrop was Manhattan, with sirens all around. During a quirky supervision session, Pierce risked a bold assertion, saying he'd figured out the meaning of the precipice and nothing Morissy could say would sway him differently. By then, they'd developed a kind of play, knowing the other would listen carefully, then refute whatever was said in an affectionate obliteration. Pierce figured his speculations would compel Morissy to correct him, and reveal the meaning of the precipice. But he was wrong. Morissy dug in and said that he had many enigmatic habits, and that Pierce must have missed all the major ones. He went on to predict Pierce would have a miserable career if he thought there was an ultimate meaning to anything.

Like a chess move, Pierce said that under normal circumstances, of course that was true, but he felt he was dead-on right in this instance and Morissy was simply having trouble with a truth he couldn't see. They had such exquisite timing. There comes a point when you challenge the master.

"OK, then, let's have it, the ultimate meaning that is," mused Morissy, leaning back, folding his fingers behind his head.

"In your lectures, you're essentially inviting the edge of everyone's mind to come close to whatever is forming in you, but you need to find an open gate. You see that some people have to look away or have to listen without looking. I've been watching everyone, including myself. Everyone has an internal preoccupation with you at the precipice, and it has the brilliant effect of making your audience face some dreaded internal equivalence of their own. People listen all the more carefully, and it forces them to be creative in reacting to the things you're actually talking about. The gate opens because you've insisted on a kind of dual awareness. It's a fantastic method."

"Oh look, our time is up for today! Mind the gap on the subway."

"I'm close, aren't I? I'm approaching that ephemeral line." A nod sufficed, and they parted. It was the start of a newfound dialogue they would never actually finish.

At the end of the memory, Pierce was relaxed enough to sample the popcorn: delicious, still warm, perfectly salted. He made a request to see Morissy in a year's time if he hadn't moved on. Plus, he needed time to make room for death to be undone. Morissy said,

"If I'm not dead for real by then, I owe a debt to you. Don't ask me to explain." There was a pale handshake, nothing close to hardy. They agreed to respect their different worlds and not exchange numbers.

Pierce came up with an idea, the kind a boy might suggest; that Morissy check for a note under a particular boulder along the Laguna Canyon Road, the same week, a year later. If no note, their meeting would have to be imaginary. Morissy retreated to his shack behind a home up on Rim Rock Canyon Road in Laguna, to his collection of local pottery and books. He'd never had a visitor and wasn't going to start now. Three or four days per week he'd go around like a doctor making his rounds, to different places selling popcorn, dispensing unexpected wisdom in a cloak of anonymity. He had a beat up truck to carry his cart around. That's as much as the pelicans could see. Pierce didn't want to count on anything with Morissy again. *Look what he's capable of,* he thought.

Chapter 5

GAME ON

Corelli must have delivered Pierce some respite from his doubts, because he was seized by the hope that Morissy would remember the calendar and check under the boulder. His note rested in a zip lock bag a few feet off a trailhead in the Laguna Canyon. It read:

Today is Monday. I just got into town as we talked about last year. Any chance you can meet me day after next at Main Beach? Say 9:00 AM. Long shot, I know. I hope you're well. H.P. Here's my cell phone in case you've joined the modern world.

Everything felt tentative and fragile, even though Morissy could have simply found his number online and cancelled. They were oddly still at play.

After leaving the note, he returned to his spot on the beach, wondering how he'd frame his need for Morissy's thoughts. In a mirror-like way, Morissy also pondered what he wanted, without coming to a conclusion. In Mexico, he spent mornings hiking and reading classics in literature, making friends, learning to cook for the first time in his life, but he never tried to purge the healer within. In the company of others, he couldn't help from making observations that might change someone's life in small moments of noticing; an unexpected compliment, a way of assuming something spoken offhand was part of a larger intention. He was good at lighting small fires in people using subtle comments and gestures. In fact, he didn't know where he was going, but never had a taste for small talk. His style followed him everywhere, caught up with him around every corner. It surprised him when he finally accepted how little had changed with his grand disguise. You think you can get away from the habit of being you, until it comes around in another form. Morissy always felt that the anomalous moment is the one remembered: a comment made during the exchange of coin, buying fruit in a market, the pattern on a scarf worn by a merchant. He would wonder if it fits the soul or has a costly meaning.

Pierce was in a different zone, and actually had an agenda. Waves tried to erase the years, but a dog barking from the boardwalk brought the tall thoughts back. Just two weeks before his trip, Pierce stood at his office window between sessions. Instead of seeing his reflection, he saw a sandy Laguna cove. In his daydream, six pelicans flew past, reminding him of the six psychotherapy patients he sees every Tuesday. Someone had been making a series of maddening hang-up calls from a blocked number every Tuesday evening. He sensed desire in the caller, couldn't say why, since no message was left. Something reminded him of words trying to form—words that were diverted before making it to the throat. That's what kept him one part curious, two parts worried.

Sometimes tensions have a name. This one didn't. No two calls were the same. He focused on background sounds coming into his answering machine, sometimes he thought he heard a sigh, followed by a click. Even René, his practice partner, listened to some of the calls, but refused to declare them sighs. She gave Pierce a bucket of why's. *Why on Tuesdays? Why keep you in the dark? Someone might want you to feel what they've been feeling, so it could be a kind of passive-aggressive test, or done to prove a futile point.* The phone company said the calls were untraceable since they were routed differently each time, from all around the world. So be it, he thought. If someone doesn't leave a message, why should he waste his time?

For a moment, he entertained that wild idea that the calls were coming from Benjamin Morissy himself. More likely it was just a robot call from a blocked number, but he couldn't be sure. If the incessant calls were coming from one of his six patients, he might take a step back and look for a pattern pointing to a rogue wave. He consulted other colleagues, even asked the Japanese lamp in his office. It bothered him that the calls always came right before he was leaving for the day. He saved his pet theory in his back pocket—that one of the six was either afraid or plenty angry. First comes structure, then content. Another thought came; someone knocks on your door and you take a minute to get there, but the person has left in frustration, thinking you're not home.

The worst moments in therapy come when you've disappeared and can't be found by your patient or even by yourself. You might be in the chair, but in a certain way, you're gone. The best moments rise like cumulous clouds in the mountains, building tension, darkening in some places, glowing in others, growing into shapes that disappear, while underneath, the rain comes slanting down.

Chapter 6

FLYING SOUTH

Getting to Southern California was always the same. Each time Pierce flew out of the central valley, time was suspended after takeoff. He'd sit on the left side of the plane to get a glimpse of the spectacular Half Dome in Yosemite. In about forty minutes, the plane veers west between Ventura and Malibu and hugs the coast not far from Long Beach Harbor, the resting place of the original Queen Mary and its stunning hardwood dance floor. All that history at sea, the grandeur docked forever as a museum. Pierce closed his eyes and thought he heard music along with the scent of perfume from elegant ladies with pearls. He was waltzing with a mysterious woman, not quite placing her accent. Other decades found him; the whispering ways of neighbors he grew up around, in insulated suburban towns. He heard news of growing racial tensions up in Los Angeles when he was just a lad, but it hardly touched Santa Ana. When he became a teen, he picked cherries one summer, and saw first hand the abject poverty of migrant farm workers. Cold war tensions made decent people paranoid, but the space race gave us hope. Kids had Hula Hoops. Adults discovered valium.

When his plane was just short of Catalina Island, it turned straight on to the mainland. He'd taken the trip a hundred times, always looking out the window to check out the waves at Newport Beach. Then the hard U-turn over Lemon Heights and down into John Wayne Airport. Pierce closed his eyes before landing, imagining the feel of saltwater, the anticipation of sand. Everyone in the airport was on a cellphone or laptop. A person reading an actual book is as rare as an orange tree in Orange County.

The landing was unusually rough and shook him quite a bit since his mind was thinking of warm sand and waves. On recent trips, he began noticing people just sitting in their cars, parked on side streets or in shopping centers or strip malls. They weren't on cell phones or making calls with a Bluetooth. No music came from radios. They didn't seem to be waiting for someone in a store. It felt like a subculture under anesthesia, waiting for something to make sense.

It's growing you know, the number of people staring forward, numb, blank, done in, stunned. Somehow they were able to pull off the manic roads and their cars were their only refuge.

He'd been staying at his deceased father's vacant home during visits, going on three years. When his father moved up north to assisted living, he refused to allow the home to be altered while he still lived. He liked the idea he might come back to inhabit it tomorrow, three years of tomorrows, so he left his tools in the garage, the magazines in piles on his desk, a disabled car in the garage, the television clicker at the side of his big red chair.

Walking into his parent's room, Pierce entered a personal museum, catching a glimpse of his high school self in photos, the water polo and swimming buddies. He bounced off these same walls in high school. How well a house remembers. In recent years he'd catch a flamenco show in Costa Mesa, a little salsa dancing up in L.A. after a Hollywood show or a visit to one of the great museums. Sometimes he went for a bit of blues in Huntington Beach. The simple moments are best; walking on the Newport Pier, peering into the buckets of people fishing. Clair, his naturalist wife, enjoyed the trips too, especially when the migratory birds were visiting the Back Bay or Bolsa Chica. This time, she's off bird watching on a retreat of her own, in Costa Rica. She sends a cell phone photo now and then; *look, a trogon, perfect yellows, startling blues, you can't believe the diversity, love. I saw an army of leaf-cutter ants at work, astonishing. They'll take over when humans are gone, having the seeming advantage of knowing where they're going.*

Pierce headed for the beach early the next morning, with swimming on his mind, along with thoughts of Morissy. On his way through the Laguna Canyon, he checked the rock and had a chill when he saw that Morissy had responded to his note, saying only, "I'll be there. Don't forget, I'm Javier now. Sick little joke. Sorry, couldn't resist."

Chapter 7

THE LAGUNA CANYON ROAD

The Laguna Canyon Road is like a person you think you know; one with a fractured past, exposed, steep in unexpected places, friendly from a distance, but up close, on any slope at all, it's easy to slip and fall. There's a patch of cactus just off the trail, and a crumble of rocks you thought were solid. There's something compelling about picking up a shell in the hills, imagining a time when you'd be underwater right where you stand. Whatever it is that rushes time along in the canyon, it stops to stare you down.

Pierce loved the last few miles of the drive. Setting aside everything else, he loved the Laguna Canyon, one of the last undeveloped areas that haven't been turned into cookie cutter homes. Even the larger cookies seem the same, with million dollar price tags and postage stamp yards. Morissy, being from the east coast, never understood the obsession with fences in front yards out west. He saw them as little compartments that seal off a life. When you describe something to Morissy, anything, he'd ask about some impressionistic detail. The presumption that a tree has any less character than one of Shakespeare's characters made Morissy frown, like you aren't looking very hard. It's why he kept a collection of smooth rocks in his therapy office in NYC, taken from various frozen ponds from his childhood. He called them his life's achievement, not because he assembled them into a collection, but because he was drawn to their character. Others would say it was his way of talking about his famous psychotherapy articles, but he never let on.

Looking up at the little caves and ragged edges of the canyon, Pierce remembered his early training with Morissy, who would wade into a case with absolutely no interest in framing the action from an elevated point of view. He would climb no hill of presumption. In fact, it took Morissy quite a while before he had something to say. Once in a while, he'd alter the pattern, demolish the rule, and surprise Pierce by diving in head first, saying something like, "You realize your sixty-year-old patient is a child speaking to you while hiding from behind the couch, don't you?" Pierce could almost visualize Morissy's provocative brow rising. He grew in the challenges, saying, "The part people come to value is the moment when I'm opening myself to expansion at the same time it's occurring in them."

There was one consistency in their supervision: Morissy delighted in allowing their discussions to include a deliberate, mingling mess of projections: those of the patient, the therapist, and himself as supervisor. He was fond of presenting riddles that had no solutions.

"We live in the convergence of mighty rivers. Seasonal forces change everything, even the shapes of riverbeds." All told, he was not one to play games. Pierce shook his head right there in the canyon. Dr. Morissy wasn't making the hang-up calls. It was not his kind of mischief.

On the last curve before coming into the city of Laguna Beach, Pierce recalled a particular moment after a long silence in a supervision session. Morissy looked through his window and lifted an unsteady hand to his chest to feel the wool of his pale blue sweater. Without giving context, he said,

"Let your patients live in you without resolution, in optimal tension. Try to keep that edge. I'll see you next time. I'm sorry to end abruptly today, I'm not feeling well."

It was the last thing Pierce remembered before the announcement came that Morissy was presumed drowned in the boating accident. He walked himself home that day instead of taking the subway up Broadway to his apartment near Columbia University. He was followed by a strange wind on a calm day. He turned to face it, but the source kept changing. The more it puzzled him, the more he realized there was no wind at all. It came from inside, something beyond the insufferable weight of grief, from a place where the self resides.

Chapter 8

FIRST SWIM

Main Beach has a singular beauty, with its long sweet crescent and fine light sand. Swim a hundred yards out and dive down fifteen feet or so, equalizing the ears, and the bottom will appear. Straight out from the main lifeguard tower, the bottom is crusty or obscure, nothing much to see, but it was a ritual. There's a scattering of small rocks and debris, maybe a few shreds of kelp moving back and forth in the surge. Of course there's no splendid reason to dive right there. Still, it's a kind of reassurance to put one's hand on the ocean floor. For Pierce, it was a way of remembering his mother, who died ten years before. She was always underneath something, the mysterious weight of her generation, the war years, the midnight shifts making bombers in the freezing Midwest during WWII, enduring her husband's expansiveness. Pierce's father was a pilot in the South Pacific during the war. After round two in the Korean War, they rarely spoke of the war years. She always had an uneasy quietness when reading, smoking her Salem cigarettes.

When you hold you breath underwater, the deeper you go the more you treasure the darkening. It's not a lonely thing, more a tribute, and a respect for the blue-gray world. In the warmer water of summer, when it's comfortable to swim out another hundred yards, other coves come into view, which is ironic, since the importance of land fades away right when you could choose to turn and see it. Better to face the horizon for a few seconds, looking out to the open sea, cold and exposed. It's the moment between birth and the very first cry.

There's only a little sting when opening the eyes underwater. In April there are very few swimmers, since it's 58 degrees. In fact, Pierce could barely stand it. He did it because it was personal. He promised himself a swim, simple as that. Without a wetsuit, hypothermia is quickly a problem. Today was a straight shot out and back; a headache was a certainty. The middle section of Main Beach is not the kelp bed forest of your dreams, that's for other beaches nearby, but kelp is coming back now that the area is a marine sanctuary. Maybe thirty years too late.

Pierce dove under his first wave with a child's sense of play. It was precisely the moment when he was able to release his troubles to the immediacy of a breaking wave. In strokes of an ocean swim, time has little meaning. You hear your breath, feel the resistance of water; it's a rendezvous, a love affair, pulling you toward the horizon, where the mind is free to remember.

Chapter 9

SECOND SWIM

Last night was a night without dreams. When he woke in his parent's home, the inland sounds haunted him, along with the screech of parrots at sunrise. All he wanted was to go back to the beach and do it all again. So he did. Plus, it was the morning he hoped to see Morissy. When he arrived, the fog was thin and wispy. On the boardwalk, between the largo and allegro of Corelli's *Concerto Grossi No. 1*, a swallow raced past his eyes and was gone. The image lingered, like the ring of a Tibetan bowl when struck with a felt-tipped mallet. It was a call to alertness, colliding with his lazy morning. The pelicans had other formations, flying in threes and fours. It was quiet except for the gulls, a sweatshirt morning. He resolved he would not judge his old friend further. Maybe just a little.

In every stroke out to the buoy, pieces of their times together came back, as if they resided in bubbles made by his own hands slicing through the cold water. When his parents died, young Benjamin learned to speak to homing pigeons. They belonged to an elderly man who lived in their building and showed him the bird language. The birds always came back; his parents never did. An aunt and uncle raised him, giving him a first-class education, and never a limit otherwise. They were kind, just shy of warm. He was a boy of boys. There was his stamp collection from Central African nations, the collection of marbles from fifty countries. Baseball cards. When he grew a few feet taller, he tried to master boomerangs.

In one of their sessions during Pierce's early training, he brought the case of a brilliant, nearly mute young man who feared all things red. He couldn't use words the way that other people could. Morissy responded by describing his own teen years, when he'd find a park at dusk to throw his wooden boomerangs until he learned their various secrets. He shunned the plastic ones. There was a painful pattern; he kept losing them, his favorites, up in trees or in a thicket. He frequently stayed long after dark, and never stopped loving the damned things. It became a topic in his personal psychoanalysis, a reverent theme, and a fantasy that if he'd been more skilled, they would not have been lost. In time, he abandoned the explanation, but what emerged was a new fear about the coming of evening, because evening meant he'd have to leave the park and go home in a state of loss. He never mastered boomerangs, but kept his hobby through college, through medical school, and finally set them aside when he thought he might become a surgeon. Finally, he circled back to the young man and his fear of red.

"Tell him about something you once dreaded. Make sure that it's absolutely true, and refuse to suggest it's a displacement of any kind. Break the rules this one time. It'll help him in the place where he needs you most. You know, for later on."

It was riveting when Morissy would offer supervision by telling a story about his own life. It showed he had nothing figured out, but he always drew Pierce into a visceral way of listening. When Pierce found himself swirling in just the right amount of alertness and confusion, Morissy would say something profound.

"You find yourself enacting a drama you've created in order to solve or explain your other dramas, the ones that are more obscure and more painful. I think that will come in your second or third year of treatment. Your young man is afraid he's making a mistake no matter what he does, and right now he fears his mistake was being born in a world that doesn't understand him. Blood, the ultimate red, is what this might be about. It's the evidence of something, but of course you don't say that to him. You never say that to him. Steer him toward art, toward large canvas paintings with oils. Let's see what he creates. Self-soothing takes mysterious paths. I can tell you this; he won't become a man interested in pastels."

For a time in his life, Morissy admitted he wasn't sure he wanted to know people. It's just that he couldn't stop himself from seeing deeply into people and finally saw his dilemma as art. When he met his wife, June, a glacial melt occurred. He rarely spoke of his marriage, but when he did, Pierce was dazzled, humbled. When June was diagnosed with aggressive cancer, Morissy spoke only once about it to Pierce.

"Take my whole life with June, imagine all our years, all our sorrows, as no more than a handful of water. You try to hold that water, knowing some drops will spill. It's not the water you drink. When one of you dies, it's the other's job to release it to a tree you planted together. This was our vow to each other, our intimacy. I'm grateful we were together long enough to sit in its shade."

Pierce remembered June as a fearless artist, certainly one to regard her marriage as private. Your mentor's marriage is not a casual matter to bring up. Pierce enjoyed seeing them together, the small touches, the way they anchored themselves in each other's glances. June was never enchanted with words, unlike her husband, and seemed to prefer the glances. Pierce wondered what their fights would be about.

Swimming back from the buoy, Pierce turned on his back for the next few strokes, thinking human nature is one thing; the story written by the self is the keener novel. In freestyle swimming, you look to where you're going; in backstroke, you see where you've been. It's good to use them both. Only a few more strokes until shore, but he paused when a school of anchovies swam near, panicked, probably being chased by a bonito. In the calm that followed, he remembered how Morissy liked to start a seminar with a provocative comment, such as the one on a steamy summer afternoon, when thunderstorms rattled the skyscrapers in Manhattan.

"Let's say you're in session with the most insightful, grounded patient in your entire practice, someone healthier than you in many respects. Let's say you're feeling comfortable in the attachment, then you suddenly realize they're desperately screaming something to you in another language, and you've entirely missed their sense of longing. It collapses your odd satisfaction in thinking you can tell the difference between their essence and their defenses. You realize you've mistaken the patina for the substance it covers and it makes your skin shudder to think you actually know this feeling from somewhere in your own life, but your mind doesn't want to bring up the memories of where. So I ask, what do we do with self-recognition and how do we use it in therapy to benefit our patient while at the same time risking our own traumatization?"

Needless to say, nobody ventured a response. Then Morissy smiled and said, "It's ok, dear colleagues, I don't expect an answer. My goal is to prepare you for the inevitability of these moments. This will be our topic for next year."

Oh, but his eyes would dance. At the end of his larger talks, he invited exactly five questions. Pierce noted these little things, having attended as many lectures as he could. In conferences, people lined up at a microphone to ask their pressing questions. Morissy would respond honestly, never making the person feel small. He insisted that the person reveal something about their way of thinking before he would comment. It had the effect of elevating the art of the question. It's why he ultimately rejected surgery as a career. Too precise for his wandering mind. He came to value curiosity, taking classes in philosophy and art. When the winds inside him settled, he chose psychiatry.

In a few years, he confided in Pierce. "You know, sometimes the one who holds back from asking a question is the one with the finest mind. I've found that the sixth person, the one who finds me alone just as I'm leaving a lecture, to be invariably compelling. Often, it's a shy, thoughtful woman sitting in a back row. She'll say something like, 'Dr. Morissy, I think I'm having an impasse with one of my patients, like the one you just described, and we're really quite stuck. I'm not sure I have a question, but I love your way of thinking.' I'd smile, and ask her if it feels like she's trying to say I've confused her, but instead she says I've inspired her. I give a little chuckle and tell her that something good will happen if she wonders privately why she uses the word *impasse*, and to look at all the assumptions she's making. I invite her to stay alongside her patient, to bring the matter front and center in a place where the therapist does not presume authority. Of course, they'll need each other to explore the matter, wherever the currents take them. It will be their walk in the woods."

Pierce responded by asking Morissy if he might simply be blind to the possibility that a lot of therapists want to be in supervision with him, or in treatment, but are too intimidated to ask. In any case, was he aware he had a gift in perceiving subtle things that most men don't notice in the slightest? Pierce had been noticing how women in particular appreciate that quality, nodding from the back of the room. Some women were quite smitten by him. Did he miss that entirely?

Morissy said he'd take the observation under advisement, which was to say he'd toss it like a paper airplane off a ten story building, and in the fall or rise, he'd be uncomfortable that Pierce accurately perceived he was exquisitely self-conscious when operating outside of a defined role. Shortly after that conversation, Morissy shared a fantasy, more like a prophesy, that he'd be content to be a giver in disguise, like a barber, a taxi driver, a man selling pretzels and hot chestnuts on the streets of Boston. He'd draw out the nature of a person with glances and small comments, then invite them down a path of self-reflection. Not as a guide, more like a muse might call you to your nature. All in all, he was eternally confused as to how he ended up being a psychoanalyst. For all his questions on the matter, he stopped needing to know. It rested in his mind like a piece of wood on the side of his yard.

Chapter 10

LANDFALL

Pierce washed ashore on a smallish wave and walked up the sand, dripping, without looking for his towel, until he was face-to-face with his old friend. Morissy was waiting for him, two coffees in hand.

"Benjamin, I appreciate you coming, thanks very much for the coffee," Pierce said. "I want you to know I can forgive lots of stuff, but I'm stumped. Maybe it's nothing, but why are you wearing a Los Angeles Angels baseball cap? How could you? You were always a Yankees fan. God knows I've faked parts of my life, and you faked your own death, so maybe we'll have lots to talk about, but dear God man, are you really an Angels fan along with your other transformations?"

"In one life there are many loves. Look, you didn't have an easy time with some theories you studied, so you switched. Why can't a person switch? Sometimes a district attorney wants to quit fighting and just sell flowers. Now I give free therapy from a popcorn cart and get to make observations to people. They pay attention because it's unexpected. I've been robbed six times on this job, and this baseball cap has saved me more often than not. OK, you got me; I wear it partly to blend in. Besides, people down here believe in their Angels. You should give it a try."

"You could have just retired, or taken time off citing medical reasons, but no, you must have known the way people would gather and speak your praises. Whatever else you tell me, don't lie."

Morissy dropped the lightness and dug his feet into the sand. When he paused, he became a statue. "I've had a year to think about seeing you again. Was there a final straw? I suppose yes. All I have is a story, not an explanation. A few months after June died, I went back to work, but made a huge mistake taking on a new couple for therapy. I got lost in the case. The wife complained of no sense of closeness, asking her husband why he doesn't pay attention while she tries to read him a Shakespeare sonnet. She really put herself into it. All he did in session was roll his eyes and say, 'here we go again.' Then the husband complained she never wanted to hear about his passion for making exotic fishing lures. She wouldn't even look at them. He found tears when he talked about them, but she said, 'So what, you won't touch me,' saying it with such venom, of course he wouldn't try to touch her. I wasn't ready for them. Every utterance was a form of payback or contempt, perfecting the art of cancelling each other. I wanted to scream to them that my wife had just died, and to get the hell out of my office. I didn't. I was too convinced of my skills from the past, when I could have helped them out of the pit. Hubris and pride did me in. When they left the sessions, I stared at the floor, thinking of a simple life in Mexico. I nursed the thought until it became an obsession, a set of actual plans.

Pierce remembered him as a man without children, first by circumstance of infertility, then two incredibly sad late miscarriages, and later by choice, deciding with his wife not to adopt. She painted oils and sang in a choir while his turbulence wove itself into genius. He was faithful to her, also to his private doubts. You could find places in his brow that looked like the glowing sun, and others that were dead end canyons. What other man fakes his death, gets a new face, then brings you coffee with a grin?

When he had his third sip of coffee, Pierce remembered the eloquent speech he made at Morissy's memorial service. He also remembered how much he wanted to un-remember it when he found Morissy was alive. He wanted to spit on the words he had uttered. Everyone in attendance – colleagues, friends, patients – wondered if they appreciated Morissy enough, recalling their favorite quotes, the hand on their shoulders, the blend of authority and humanity, the gifts they'd received. Morissy had more to say.

"At home, I kept seeing my wife's image at my empty table, and pretty much everywhere else, even in the bathroom mirror. I should have taken a few months off. When you let someone in your practice, they're part of your interior life, the liminal places, the places you don't control. I told most patients I'd had a personal loss, explaining my absence, and accepted their care and concern. But in the end, I abandoned everyone, starting with myself. I should have been a surgeon. When surgeons are suicidal, they're definitive about it. Look at the mess I've made. As far as I know, that couple stayed together, guarding their misery like wolves. Sorrow is not the same as depression. Sorrow has a taste, a slow, melodious resolve to engulf you. Depression is more of an abyss." He started to shake like he was the one who was cold.

"How was your swim?" He asked.

"It was bracing, really stupid in fact. Look at me, I'm blue from the cold and I didn't have to do this. I appreciate you saying something about what happened. I would have tried to help, you know. I missed June too. I'm only going to say this once, you took a coward's path and it locked a lot of good people out of the chance to take care of you." Pierce had a thousand other questions in mind, but none that found a voice. Morissy nodded and squinted at the sun as if to punish his eyes.

The words that stung were said and done, and Pierce asked a special favor. "I'd like to take you to the beaches I love, where I've been going since childhood. Each one has become a thinking place. It might feel like the walks we used to take during supervision. I see six people every Tuesday in my practice, and I think one of them has been calling and hanging up. It's getting weird. It's under my skin. Since you know me from the old days, I'm hoping you'll see something I can't. There may be no mystery to solve, but I've always valued your thoughts. I'll warn you, one beach is where I go to think about the patient I inherited from your practice."

"Yes, of course, but remember, I sell popcorn now, that's all. You're talking about Ava, aren't you?" Pierce threw a broken shell into the brine, spinning it into a wave. It was his way of saying *yes, that's her.* They got into Pierce's rental car and floated on down the Pacific Coast Highway. Parking is easy in April.

Chapter 11

PEARLS AND AGATES

The beaches at the ends of Pearl and Agate Streets are known to hypnotize. The men stood on the overlook while the sky finished polishing the morning. Pierce surprised himself, jumping right in.

"This view is where I think of my first patient every Tuesday. Kiko isn't his real name, but we can borrow freely from disguises. Kiko has a story beyond my experience, one foot in his Japanese heritage, the other in America. He came here when he was twelve, now he's thirty, with a solid job, very bright, but unsure of what he wants from people and blocked when he looks inside. He could have looked for a Japanese therapist, but he wants to see me, a thoroughly American white guy. I'm swimming in a culture I don't really know, in traditions I never lived. Of course I ask him to educate me."

Morissy bent down and picked up a small branch left behind by a gardener. With his other hand, he reached for a pebble shaped like a sphere. "Yes, go on. You know I like to touch things as I listen."

"His family is mystifying, even to him. He tells me he's embarrassed to talk about their habits and moods because it would feel too close to criticizing, a forbidden idea. I remind him there's a difference between describing his own experience and judging others. He's not so sure. He wasn't proud of the way his father treated his mother, but told me it was worse two generations before. I see how treacherous it is for him to claim an observation. He speaks of ancestors, but knows little about their internal worlds. All roads lead to shame. He could move to Japan; it's not a matter of language, which he's mastered. He feels he'd have a rougher time there. Besides, he's drawn to Latin women. So I come to these two beaches below us, one braced by a bookend of rocks, the other open-ended. Pearl to the left of us, Agate to the right. We've been meeting for two years. The hours in therapy seem more about tone than content."

Morissy raised his head to speak. He'd been listening keenly while looking at the sign that names the beach. It's a sign of welcome that also comes with a warning, not to take anything away, to leave everything as you find it. Morissy's mind was always churning with the mixed nature of things. It felt like the old days. Morissy repeated one of his favorite lines.

"What did he say about his reasons for coming?"

"He came because he fears he drives people away, and he's predicted that will be my fate too. At first, I resented being tested, being cast in his self-defeating assumption. I feel shame-traps at every turn. Kiko won't talk about emotions, but shows me pieces of his will. A late cancellation here, a smirk there, a genuine moment disavowed, but he keeps returning, demanding a kind of formality that's civil but tightly wrapped. I believe he's showing me both his constraints and his desire to be recognized outside the constraints, like he needs to see if I can survive something he knows somatically, something that you can't explain in other ways. Doing therapy with people from other cultures is the hardest of all. Of course, there's plenty of transference at play, the kinds that feel familiar, but there's cultural transference and cultural counter-transference too. Americans are obsessed with individuation. To him, it's not the goal. At least Kiko and I can talk about culture openly, with irony and sometimes humor. But I can't tell if he's just accommodating my ignorance when he really wants to correct me. I've never been to Japan. People tell me they can visit many places there, but much of the society is off-limits, highly guarded. He readily agrees, and says that even though he speaks Japanese, the gestures are always daunting. He'd quickly be seen as foreign. He told me there's a whole universe of politeness, ritual, and power, that he's not at home anywhere he goes."

Morissy closed his lips tighter than a clam, and opened them to claim a slow deep breath.

"Here's one way I see your work, and I might be horribly wrong. I think Kiko has rage where he thinks he's supposed to have logic by now, and you, being a kind soul but not living in his shoes, try to use logic and permissiveness to appreciate the identity he's having a rough time claiming. I see a bus on a road too narrow, but I'll bet he passes the hours paying attention to how the office looks; not you in it, just the office, and there's an odd sense of danger for him to need you. It's not so simple as evasion. To speak directly to you will not come easily. It will be a triumph when it happens."

"I'm on the lookout for that. He'll talk about a pile of books, a portrait, or an empty coffee cup. If I say something, anything, he withdraws the observation. It bothers him that I think he's talking about something important. But in truth, I do think it's important. If I push, he smears himself with criticality. Clam shells come to mind."

"What do you notice physically in yourself."

"I'll start to clutch my knee, but I end up soothing it instead, because something has called me into tension. I'm being deflected from my own associations, and when I think into it, Kiko won't call me back into the room. It's not easy for me to go most of the session in silence like some therapists seem to do. He's perfectly capable of that, like he's been doing it since childhood, respectfully waiting for a response, probably seething inside. I try to respect the wounds he doesn't put into words. If I ask him about emotions, he thinks there should be a right answer. He recently said he wished the room could be darker and I asked him if he'd like me to turn off the light so the natural light from outside would be enough. He said yes, and I did it. It seemed to help. The ability to sit with each other took an exquisite turn. It's been one of our best moments. I think it was because he asked for something and I simply gave it to him. It must have been very risky for him."

Morissy responded in his mercurial way by offering lines from a poem written by one of his enigmatic students about the inner experience of a woman waiting for her therapy session. In the poem, you get to see her thoughts:

You don't want light to find you
Or the chair to make a sound
Or the angled window to be so perched
It easily reveals your outline

"Yes," said Pierce, "that's it. The light has to offer the right mix of privacy and illumination. It was his request that mattered. I've missed our talks, you know."

Morissy made a little bow. "Maybe I'm a little like Kiko, a little like you as well. I remember myself from before. My disguise fooled the world, but never me. No wonder therapists go mad."

"Not for me to judge," said Pierce. "You could have had an angry suicide, but you took pains to make it seem like you died doing something you loved. Look, you're being a dope. You're not like other people in this field. You're an artist, creative, humble and wise. Show me a person who isn't flawed? Back to us! Forget my case if you like, forget trying to help. What do you see in these beaches? When I come to this overlook I end up restless and unsettled and walk down to Arch Cove, just out of sight."

"Who says you have a problem with Kiko? It's a problem you're having with you," said Morissy, walking over to smell a bougainvillea even though he knows damn well they don't have a detectible fragrance. Pierce loved being in Morissy's brilliant presence again.

"Look at me," Morissy said, "disappointing myself by thinking that because the bougainvillea is so lovely, it should also have a beautiful fragrance. It's like asking it to be a gardenia, which it can never be. A gardenia draws you in and rewards you with its dreamy fragrance for an encore. If you pick one, it turns brown in a matter of hours. But we're not looking at a gardenia. When you step back from a bougainvillea, you see the beauty of the cluster. What you have with Kiko is a luminous cluster. You'll be more helpful by seeing if you can stay with him along the narrow mountain terrace he's showing you. On parts of it you have to walk single file, then later side-by-side. There's plenty of good tension in your therapy. Tone is a language of its own. He's giving you a roadmap."

Morissy swept his outstretched arm across the scene, unleashing a fanciful tale.

"I liken this place to the contrast between a mother and father, how they reside in the same child. Being a therapist has changed with the times. Remember the era when we thought the point of therapy was to integrate everything that is split off, validate every piece, trace every origin, and deliver it all back as a package of pseudo-understanding? I think it's more honest to say we live in shared conundrums of the impacts we have on each other in the good old *here and now.* I think that's what's disturbing you. You've tapped into Kiko's sadness about the theme of renunciation, like he feels he has to devalue one of his parents, parts of his ancestry, parts of his first culture, and you've come to represent the container for all this and you're very close to his internal world; a painful world where he feels he has to choose. Which will it be, Pearl or Agate? Refuse to choose. Take a walk on both beaches. That's my thought."

Pierce nodded, looking over at a group of succulents, trying to appreciate them exactly as they are. "Yes, of course," he said, kicking a pebble, a little more confused than before.

Morissy was on a roll. "Usually, when parents divorce and the child is young, the child feels the divorce is their fault and they end up identifying with one parent and devaluing the other, but eventually, curiosity about the absent parent comes around to visit. It may be decades later. They'll start remembering they were told to feel one way or another, and it won't sit well. Then it's crunch time. All I'm saying is the freedom to attach in your own way is hard won, harder for some than others. I think it was a breakthrough that you simply turned the light off in your office. See how I get carried away. I think that when he was twelve, he left for America with one parent, and he's still having a rough time because nobody asked him what that did to him. Now, can we go down the stairs?"

"Of course. I've always appreciated seeing where you're curious to go. What do you make of that arch over there, the one they call 'keyhole?'"

"It's a portal to another world, of course. Who can prove otherwise? I'm a big fan of science fiction, in case you don't remember. That land bridge makes a frame, big as a church door. I'm drawn to the rock that juts out into the ocean."

They walked down to the beach at the end of Pearl Street, past the empty lifeguard tower, right to the edge of water.

"By the way," Pierce asked, "how the hell did you guess that Kiko is still haunted by the divorce of his parents and how his Japanese ancestors are calling to him from his past? I didn't tell you about the divorce, the custody battle, the ocean between his mother and father, or why he chose to work with an American male therapist."

"You supplied the imagery, I'm taking my cues from you. Sometimes I'm so far off it's laughable. Don't look to me for answers; you'll be disappointed. You know, young people are compelled to go out on that bridge over the portal, to the slippery edges, even at their peril. We were like that once."

They turned and walked north, to the open stretch of Agate Street Beach where skimboarders were busy casting their magic blankets, pressing and curling on slicks of water while friends looked on with approval. The world condenses to a five second ride, at best a little longer.

Pierce was visited by a memory of his own. This is where he came at seventeen, when he'd just broken up with a girlfriend.

He could have chosen the cove but it would have closed him in. Something more exposed was the better mirror and waves kept him occupied while the facts settled in. He didn't mention the memory to Morissy, but told him something new, looking back at the arch from a greater distance.

"I'm with you. The heartening bit is how the rock persists, jutting into the sea. It feels like defiance, like the rock is saying, *come at me, I'm here to stay.* Kiko comes at me like waves, always returning, always finding out I'm still here."

Morissy listened with the grin of a Cheshire cat. "You think too much, probably don't eat nearly enough popcorn." Then he said, "I see what you mean," and touched Pierce lightly on the shoulder.

It's true that you can just keep walking north from Agate Street Beach, especially at low tide. You can walk on and on, while the names of the streets above are changing. The two stopped to look at a woman running backward, trying to catch her wild child in a photo as he ran toward her in the wet packed sand. Up on dry sand, slumps of kelp marked the last high tide. A million flies with translucent wings peeled away as the boy ran past. Other children came to watch the spectacle. Soon everyone was fascinated with the kelp and the flies, tearing off pieces, holding them up to the light, popping the bulbs that allow the canopy to float, making strands into hats and beards and skirts. The mother declared it all to be a slimy mess and begged them to leave the kelp alone. Still, she laughed and took another photo. Come on a clear November evening, and you'll see sun setting directly behind Catalina Island.

Pierce was still cold from his morning swim and stretched out in the warm sand, resting his chin on his hands after pulling the sand to his chest; an old tradition. Morissy finally sat as well, cross-legged, head in palms, and closed his tired eyes. They surrendered to the lapping waves and the sounds of children laughing.

Pierce woke first, and looked over at his old friend, who was breathing hard, as if he'd been chased in a dream. If he'd had a towel or a blanket, he would have placed it over Morissy's shoulders, but the thought was enough to rouse him.

Pierce brought up his second Tuesday patient.

"This comes to me now, and for some reason this stretch of beach always does this to me. I can't stay awake here for long. My patient, Fay, puts me to sleep in curious ways, like I've been drugged and it's not a bad thing, like I need to be asleep or she won't tell her story. When I wake, I can't remember what we've said, it's like catching every third word in the wind. There's magic dust in her voice, which ranges from soft to gravel, but the pacing of her words is like a metronome. I'm hardly in the room with her before it starts. The sounds in the office – the ventilation fan, the muffled noise of traffic outside, even the doors opening and closing in other offices – won't shake us from our two-step dance. But of course we're not actually touching each other. I wonder what I am to her, who I am to her? Her story isn't sad in the common ways. In fact the lack of sadness is what seems to bother her."

Morissy laid back into the sand using his elbows, and pulled his baseball cap down low.

"Sleep is a tricky business, and Fay is very powerful. I feel her influence through you. We're used to people being numb after trauma, but her trauma seems to be that of not being recognized, and not expecting anyone to really see her deeply, so her superpower is to put others to sleep. I imagine she came to realize both her fear and her power after some pivotal event, but it may just be my need to have a fantasy, a wish to know what I can't, except through my own variations. I don't think we can completely sort out the difference. Now, when she's close to being recognized, she's not sure what to do with it. It rattles her that you seek to know where she goes, even more that you care about the places she's been. My God, I see what you mean. She brings such anesthesia."

Pierce continued, "When I'm with her, we're on different sides of a raft floating down a quiet river under a peach-colored sky. When I speak, she nods. When she speaks, the words barely make it through the short distance between us. In my office, she'll take the chair one day, the couch the next. I'm starting to notice things. She wears a yellow skirt on days when she softly cries, and when she wears the blue dress, she offers carefree anecdotes of people at work or in a store. She's never critical of others, just offers vignettes that amuse her. I'll ask about her marriage, and she'll say, 'Oh that, it's fine, I have no complaints.'"

Morissy listened equally to the gulls overhead and to Pierce. "I can't help you on this one, I'm sorry. I've just had a daydream of my wife, June. She came to me with a string of pearls, and they suddenly broke and scattered on the hardwood floor of our apartment. She never wore pearls in our entire marriage. Now I wish I'd bought her some. In my daydream I gather them one by one and place them in a delicate box and promise to take them to a jeweler to be re-strung. I want her to wear them when we go to see the Julliard String Quartet playing Brahms, her favorite. She would look magnificent wearing them. I love that I've played a part in her feeling beautiful. She smiles. Why didn't I go to the ends of the world to bring her that set of pearls? I can see her wearing them now, in her indigo dress, hair all up, with a hairpin made of ebony. What did you say about your patient? Something about a raft? Did you say you have a fantasy of dancing with her? She's oddly present in me, something about the way you bring her here, the way you call her Fay. Part of you is always trying to listen to her. It's just that she's in the key of G and you play a B-flat instrument. Don't give up transposing."

They sat a while longer and dozed for an unknown time. Pierce realized he'd been blocking the flow of images that come along with Fay, how she'll skip along the surface and dance through therapy hours in soft and pleasant ways. He'll try to stay awake next time and pay more attention to his daydreams.

"She has a way of glossing over childhood, like she never had one, and perhaps she didn't. Something about her dresses stands out, the way she'll change chairs and say nothing about it. She always seems perched on a curb, confident that if she raises a hand, a car will arrive to whisk her to the next moment."

It came to Pierce in the brine that Fay allows him to know her only in certain ways: everyday anger dismissed too quickly, rations of muted pity, a preference for daisies over roses. She could be the lace at the hem of the universe, but not say anything about her marriage. Now that he's opening to her language, she comes to him like the pearls in Morissy's daydream, scattered in his mind. He has a daydream too, to build a structure wide enough within himself so Fay can unfold, like this beach. He'll need the beach to give her a place to visit her unclaimed memories and not need dissociation. It will not be easy. He and Morissy drifted north for a hundred yards before they could think again.

Chapter 12

VICTORIA

In another hour, Pierce had an impulse to take Morissy to Victoria Beach, walking under the Pacific Coast Highway, past a dozen upscale homes to the to the start of the long descent. Victoria is perfect for swimming parallel to shore, a unique serenity once you're out beyond the waves. On the beach, the pristine sand seduces you to stay, but if you walk around the rocks to the north, an old seawall awaits your exploration, with remnants of a saltwater swimming pool. There's a fairy tale house, with a lawn right down to the tide pools, a decorative little lighthouse too. Victoria is wide, un-crowded, where the afternoon light keeps the bluffs in a constant display of oranges and browns, even pink when the clouds are right. Even when it's mid-afternoon, there's an unearthly glow. Most of the year, it's not safe for body surfing, no angle, with an abrupt shore break, almost as bad as Camel's Point or Aliso. But when conditions are right, it's exquisite for skimboarding. Surfers try the south end, with varying success.

Their descent to the beach was solemn. Pierce couldn't help himself out of his own frame, so it was totally unnecessary when he said the obvious.

"This beach is unusual, worth the stairs and the long approach. By the way, I want your job, or something similar. I would like to be the ice cream man in a little truck with a bell on it. I'd make children happy."

Then he said, "This beach is like Belinda, my third Tuesday patient. Her waves break constantly on my shore. She's elegant, can be fierce, much like here, and after a storm, it rattles me how lush her anger feels. She wants me to be the personal caretaker of a hidden treasure, but I have to get past the dragon that guards the entrance. She seems to think I can transform her into someone more at peace, but I saw right from the beginning she's the gifted one, not me. She'll make a slight demand, and then catch herself like a person turning left when they started to turn right. It's strange; when I'm with her I'm able to be more patient than I've ever been. She speaks with her hands, then rests them on the sides of her chair as if to ask them what they've been saying. If I'm quiet, she'll say exactly what she's seeing. But the first part of every session feels more like raw endurance."

He knew that Morissy was listening, although he seemed far away. Pierce softened his description, suddenly unaware of what he was trying to say.

"It's the same with these shifting sands at Victoria. Belinda brims in radiated heat all summer, her emotions are naked in winter, like cottonwoods along the river up in Sacramento. You can see every little stem. I think I know her better when I come here. There's a wall of sand from the last high tide; each day a different sculpture, a different terrace. In my twenties, I'd come here and jump over the edge like a child, and lean into the soft bank of sand until I almost disappeared. The berms can be six feet high. It's too hot in summer to cross the beach barefoot without sandals. At other times, being with Belinda is like one of those dreams where you take twenty steps and get nowhere. It's one of my dreaded lifeguard dreams. I'm running to get to the water for a rescue, but the sand won't release my feet. I'm stuck in slow motion. She's a landscape portrait that never dries on canvas. Her colors can't be named."

"You can stop using the name Belinda, my good friend, I know this lady," Said Morissy. "You're speaking of Ava, my patient that continued with you when I left the scene? Generous that you use the name Belinda, a favorite set of sounds."

With that, Morissy slumped to the sand and covered his face, not wanting to pull up the image, the memories, but Pierce asked him to listen, and reassured him he didn't want to throw Ava in his face, that he only wanted to make the elephant leave the room. He told Morissy in the softest tones possible that he was still caring for her. He said it in the midday sun, exposed, halfway between stairs and water.

"Yes, Ava is still with me, and she remembers all your ways of helping her navigate her storms. I've never seen such pure emptiness when I first started seeing her. I was a mannequin to her, a link she couldn't use. She only knew that you and I knew each other, but not the extent. You know, it's funny, like having a big brother means you will always be the little brother. Ava will always see me as your apprentice, mining the hills for gold you've hidden in me. It's taken a long time for her to allow me to be myself. It's easy to see traces of you in her. You were more helpful to her than you might have guessed. She's adopted some of your mannerisms, especially the ones that soothe her, like the way she brushes an unwanted image off her knee, or touches her brow, or uses her finger to caress her hair, just the same as you. She has the capacity to love others. When she cares about someone, there's no longer the element of sabotage. She's real to herself from moment to moment, mood to mood. Before, as you well know, she could barely tolerate being alive. Everything was too painful; every hopeful moment was a prelude to a loss. I thought you'd like to know she's coming along. The effects on me are complicated, obscure."

Morissy shook the sand from his socks, and then took them off along with his shoes, as if the bare sensory truth called him to leave his disguise.

"I must thank you for caring for her when I could not. I couldn't see what I meant to her, not in the final year when I was so consumed. Of course she knew something was pounding away at me, something I tried to deny. She followed me into my own depression. She was much braver, much stronger than I realized. It wasn't just my troubles; it was her closeness to my aloneness that I couldn't let her see. Now I know she wasn't as afraid of it as I. There's an irony for you. She was trying to show me how to carry it. She's been doing it all her life. You've helped her not to be destructive."

"It's odd to be survivors. It's not just about guilt. I think we're always floating in afterimages, clinging to memories like driftwood. Ava and I have a joke that's not really a joke. *What would Dr. Morissy say?* One thing I know for sure is that psychotherapy has little to do with one person drawing the other out of a dark forest. Do you think she's the one calling me then hanging up? Did you have something like that going on when you were seeing her? She seemed to know your troubles, although she never told me how she knew. She knows you had a great fondness for her. She allows it to still feel present."

"You know, she always said she was born in the wrong century, fancied herself in Ireland by the sea, around 1800. My wife used to say I belonged in another century too, but never said which one, just that I might be restless anywhere and needed to be near water. Ava would love this beach. She's the kind who could sit right where we are now, in a winter storm with a parka over her head, the only person on the beach, listening to the pelting rain. Tell me, was Ava angry at first? When I disappeared."

"Were you angry when June died?" Pierce shot back with a bit of intended acid.

"Sorry, I withdraw the question. I've lost the right to ask."

I must guard Ava's confidence on the details. But, yes, it was one of many weights she carried. I can only imagine how it was for you when June was gone but your patients were still sitting in front of you. Ava had you figured out, you know. It's hard to get mad at a person who dies in a sudden accident. You always remember the last time you met, the small gestures, the omissions."

Morissy listened as keenly as he could, adding, "There's something I should tell you. When Ava was in treatment with me, I received a few letters without any return address, three in the last year we met. Inside, there was only a blank page, neatly folded, like a letter might be there, but instead there was only an empty page. I thought she might have been sending them, her way of inviting me to say what I couldn't say in sessions. But it felt childish, unlike her bold manner otherwise. It got me to thinking. The mystery was never solved. I had twenty people in therapy at the time, and I was patient, oh so patient."

"If it's her, I like the empty page better than hang-up calls. I've had similar things happen before, but usually it's someone who's angry or sarcastic, someone saying I've got a blind spot a mile wide, that I'm the dumbest therapist who ever lived, etc. Who am I to argue?"

Morissy turned away from the water. "Here's something I've never told anyone. I stayed late in my office a few nights and actually wrote on the blank pages. I thought it would bring me close to something important. Poetry came out, a haiku, a paragraph of prose. All of it was lush and uninhibited. I gave myself permission. I suppose it was a little tit for tat, since I always encouraged my patients to find creative expression. Once, I wrote about Ava as if I saw her through a waterfall. I think it helped me appreciate the passion that a blank page offers."

"I've breached her confidentiality telling you this much," said Pierce, who was moved to tears himself. "You're welcome to say more, but I can't tell you more about her treatment with me. Promise you'll never try to contact her. I hope you understand."

Morissy fell silent for a few tense moments. "Of course. I'm glad she's seeing you. You know, there's the beauty of a desert here, even though we're on a beach. My wife June always wanted me to see the shapes she saw in her driftwood discoveries. She found them much more interesting than shells. She'd walk with a shell long enough to know it, and wouldn't say what she was thinking. Then, in ten or fifteen minutes, she'd return it to the sand. It was a small crime if I asked her about it, but if I asked about driftwood, she was never short of words. That's marriage for you. One door is always open, another eternally closed. It's strange how I became close enough to Ava that I could see an alternate reality, a portal, as if I was married to her and June was coming to me for therapy. There were times in sessions when Ava joked about doing the dishes with me, having small skirmishes, like who would wash and who would dry? Of course we were enacting these things in our work, finding other ways to frame it. We had brief hugs when her dog suddenly died, when her daughter was hospitalized. One was longer, and neither of us seemed to know what we were saying in the moment. Never a kiss or caress, but I'd be lying if I said it was nothing. I remember her as the desert in bloom that moment."

Pierce took a look at a fishing boat on the edge of the horizon.

"If I imagine camping here, the night would deliver dreams of my wife Clair, where love is slow and the waves can be close or distant. In our long-term work, we come to know each other more than we bargain for. In the big picture, I think we only want to live in our relationships, not explain them."

Morissy had a tear running down his cheek by then, surprised at what he'd said. For all his private grieving, it had been years since he'd talked out loud about anyone he cared about. Not directly, not like this. In the past, so many people had elevated him, he came to believe he always had to say something important to a person in a quandary. Pierce sensed it, and returned the gift of a hand, to help his friend get up from the swallowing sand.

"I remember you and June used to love the tide pools on every beach vacation you ever had, watching the action of crabs and anemones, all the tiny fish. I love them too, the micro-worlds revitalize us somehow, give perspective, and shake off the weight of self-importance." Morissy just nodded, with no desire to deepen his loss by approaching the tide pools.

Pierce moved on. "The sand here is the most sensual I know. Fifty yards back from shore and you can easily forget the ocean. When I come here, or to Thousand Steps Beach, there's a stunning sense of isolation. I suppose it's what I come for. No sounds of traffic on the highway. I don't know if my thoughts are even my own. It's surprising how easily I give myself over."

Morissy shook off the heaviness. "There are too many kinds of hunger, but I'm thinking of the one you can do something about. Something became too painful for me in that year when I took my boat ride. It wasn't just that I went back to work too soon. The blade of a surgeon changed my face but the rest of me stayed in the mirror."

"To me, you are as vivid as before. I hope you don't doubt that. There's a good veggie sandwich up at *The Stand,* on Thalia Street. The avocados are exquisite." Pierce thought he could minimize what he just heard. It didn't work. Sometimes the best you can do is to make room for another person to be sad. In their own way, of course, not yours.

"I'd like to stay here a while, and catch up with you in two days if you're game. How about meeting at Shaw's Cove at 9:00 A.M. on Thursday. The part he couldn't say was how deeply he missed their bittersweet honesty.

"I never tried to go back to NYC," said Morissy. "It's something I've pondered for years. It would have been too risky, too crushing. The city follows me around and it does no good to draw a curtain across the decades. It seems I'm expert at expelling myself. I can't even work my popcorn job at the Orange Circle anymore, or the Huntington Pier or the base of Newport Pier. I never bothered to get a license for my roving enterprise. Now I'm looking for inland parks in Fullerton and Garden Grove. I end up getting kicked out wherever I go, but a two-week stay is often long enough. Of course I can go up to Venice Beach for a lark, but I'd have to stay on the move and I'm getting too old for that scene. I'm sure I'm enacting something over and over, so save your comments just in case you're about to speak the obvious. Just a rebel, I suppose."

When they parted, Morissy took the stairs in a labored way, resting every third step as if the weight he carried came in threes. Pierce couldn't get used to the plastic surgery that altered the face of his friend, since it altered the original grin. It was odd, since the intention behind the smile was still there.

Chapter 13

THE SANTA ANA WINDS

Pierce got a second coffee and drove back up the highway, taking a walk along the bluffs at Heisler Park. He didn't mean to evoke pain in his old friend, but he also knew it was inevitable. It's true, nobody got him thinking the way Morissy did. His cell phone buzzed. It was Clair, texting him she'd seen twenty-seven birds that day in Costa Rica, ten were new on her life list. Honeycreepers, toucans, a mot mot. *Having a great time, I hope you are too, my love.* It was easy to respond to her about the beaches, not the man he was with. *I ran into an old friend, don't worry, not an old lover. You are my great love. The beaches are exquisite as usual. I've got a rare bird for you: it's me!*

As he stood looking at the hillside, tiny fluffs of air arrived in soft persuasion, lifting and dropping the locks of his thick sandy hair. A person watching might have declared it was only a flurry, not a gust that finally succeeded in drawing Pierce's eyes to the top of the swaying palms. A gentle invitation calls for gentle seeing. The skin knows it first: a drying of the air, a prickly sensation, a soft broom dusting the whole of your being, signaling a change in the weather.

For the first hour or so, it's hard to tell the direction of the wind. You recall the last time, and remember what's coming. The skin remembers. It's a Santa Ana wind, blowing from the east. Pressure builds in the Great Basin, seeking a way out, craving the low pressure over the sea; the old story, air rising, losing moisture, heating up under an invisible dome, barging through the mountain canyons. The only questions are how hard, how long? They can be gentle or fierce, and the first hints don't tell. They can bring the rage of a canyon fire or tease like a fickle beast. If the winds arrive when winter is in charge, the season yields in a matter of hours. Trees are easily uprooted and the dust can be so thick, you think you're in Morocco. But it's often pristine at the shore.

If you lose your hat on a bluff, it can sail two hundred yards before finding its watery grave. If you needed a thick sweater the day before, now you can wear a bathing suit. The high desert is an angry adolescent, fed-up, hungry and demanding, running off to the coast. Suddenly, you can see Catalina Island. In just the right moments, you can see the ugly orange haze of civilization in the very act of receding. The astonishing part is you thought it was reasonably clear even before the unveiling.

On the bluffs above Picnic Beach, Pierce was relieved to be alone. He couldn't filter the old days through the lens of the present tense. He was thinking how Morissy was famous to his students for his pensive backward leans, his tilt toward the ceiling, with hands covering his eyes in sudden associations, followed by a brushing of his hair. He preserved the motion long after there was much hair to brush, using a comb of fingers just to feel his skin. Previously, he let his hair fall without intervention, like it represented the return of an irascible thought, an object that couldn't fit in a drawer. He'd stop what he was doing, smile at nothing in particular, and then resume his lecture.

In Pierce's memory, Morissy never asked a person why they did something, since he presumed it was either a kind of self-soothing, a quiet scream, or something in-between. Morissy supervised his earliest psychotherapy cases; the ones that stay fresh no matter how many years have passed. There were other supervisors too, shapers you might say: the incredible Elizabeth Mars, who had a mischievous brilliance, always challenging him to go deeper into the smallest moments. And the quiet Oliver Falkner, a genius that recognized the internal world with such clarity and common sense he had a unique way of inviting his patients to set aside resentments and take the path of agency. Ernesto Madrid gave him the perspective that every human variation was linked in history to traits that somehow survived. He'd challenge you to know the hardest parts, even the floundering remnants, as parts of a passion play. He'd ferret out the choices a person didn't think they had. Stephanie Abramson was so intrigued and dumbstruck by the ironies of human paralysis she helped Pierce see traps in the woods and reminded him to be tenacious as he approached the suffering mind. Like Morissy, his best supervisory thoughts came while he was walking.

The shapers went on and on, but it was Morissy who held court in his office during lunch and in walks in Central Park. The best times were in late October, among the leaves, the reds and furtive oranges. Come to think of it, Morissy typically had a bag of popcorn. Pierce looked forward to their meetings, often skirting the issue of how his therapies were acting upon him. It was a little like being a son, where you look forward to someone being home, but it doesn't occur to you what it was like for your parents to raise you. That part comes when you're older.

Morissy would have none of this skirting business, and took the attitude that his offerings were no more on-target than Pierce's, so he asked Pierce to talk about whatever came in view. He'd always say something unexpected.

"I defer to your more recent adolescent experience on this one." He could be gleeful, looking straight ahead no matter what was actually in front of him. By Friday afternoon, the flowers in his office always looked a little sad. He used to say, "I won't throw away a thought or an observation even when it's no longer fresh. I swear it's not neglect."

He used to say, "You'll find that most therapists have their favorite cup present, whether it has anything in it or not. I'm that way with coffee: hot, cold or none. It's more about the cup." He never felt the years gave him the gift of clarity, but knew how to weather storms of affect and doubt, when to pause and when to offer a safety net. His belief that Pierce would find his way was comforting beyond measure to the new psychologist. It felt less and less like training, more about someone encouraging his style, with no interest in making him a clone. They shared a mutual curiosity about how their patients found them behaving. That's when their stories came out of the barn. Resolution was not the point, only travels.

Upon meeting again, Pierce didn't have the guts to tell Morissy that he inherited a box of notes that never made it to a clinical chart. They were his poetic notes, his associations, images, and vignettes. No names were on the pages to identify anyone, not a clinical term among them. There were hundreds of scribbles in longhand. He remembered a few that stood out.

"Today, I'm the table in her study; the one she loads up with books, a coat, and gloves. She closes the door so nobody will enter the room, leaving me there while she attends a party. I can hear her laughter. I want to join her but I'm only a table in her study."

Another one caught Pierce's eye. "Today my excellent man has turned himself into a jellyfish, with long fluorescent tendrils, moving toward the depths to catch some bits of plankton. He's showing me what he has to do to stay alive. I try to follow him, but I, being human, must come up for air. I dive again and find him. Never have I felt so guilty for being human."

Pierce thought many times of bringing the notes to a bonfire pit on one of these trips, near the Balboa pier, to give them a proper ending. The ashes could fly on a moonless night in blackened carbon offerings. Better first to offer them to their author, just not yet. Things are way too fragile. Another note floated from the sky. "I've just met an injured gull caught in a fishing net. I think I can free him easily and he'll take it from here. Probably he'll come for three sessions, but it might be four, or four hundred. Whatever comes of our work, I must be careful not to become the net."

Pierce had taken to writing his own impressionistic versions of his work, following Morissy's lead, since it loosened up his mind and kept his old friend close.

He started thinking about the subtle moments in psycho-therapy. There's always curiosity about small things that might suffer an overlay of meaning; a scarf left on a bookcase shelf, a check left unsigned, a sigh where none had gone before. Of course there are louder messages, a missed appointment right after a turbulent one. The person who says, "Oh, do we have our appointment on Tuesdays? Funny how I've been thinking we were on Wednesday all this time." Sometimes, it's as if the previous session never happened. Pierce loved it when someone changed chairs or tried another section of the couch without comment. Last year, a young woman slid to the floor, crossed her legs and drew them tightly to her chest. Prelude to a soliloquy. His only wisdom was to remain quiet and make room inside himself.

Chapter 14

INLAND CHORES AND WANDERINGS

In the morning, Pierce took the last loads of his deceased father's clothes to Goodwill. The large plastic bags were bulging and he had trouble stuffing them into the tiny trunk of his rental car. But it was high time. Creating space was the goal and also the way forward. He included a pile of cardigan sweaters along with twenty or so handkerchiefs and a surprising number of shoelaces. He found dozens in his father's top drawer; even the tattered ones had been saved. Pierce never tried to make sense of the contents of the drawer before, or his own top drawer for that matter. One might draw a map of the contents, but we're too busy living.

His father must have started keeping shoelaces before he joined the Marines, a legacy from the time when all gentlemen owned wooden shoe trees for their black wing tips and had a collection of neckties that spanned the decades, wide to thin, cotton to silk. There was a small box with cufflinks, but the stronger statement was an assortment of short-sleeved shirts, a monument to his resolve never to return to Chicago and Long Island and Omaha. All his casual shirts were plaid; none had stripes. Only the dress shirts were plain. Like he made a rule.

Pierce kept the war medals and three generations of oil cans from the garage, with their fantastic reservoirs and spouts. In other drawers he found a piece of his Irish grandmother's red hair, and photos of his mother as a young woman of eighteen, when his father went off to WWII the day after their wedding. Nobody complained back then. Pierce kept a clipping that his father saved, yellowed from age, from an old newspaper that didn't have a reference. It read, *Life is but a scented rendezvous.* Some day he'd track down the author. He didn't know much about his great grandfather, but inherited a watch that still works, made of coin silver, a Seth Thomas, heavy as a cell phone. The man had eight siblings, supervised coal miners in Pennsylvania. His side hailed from Wales; grandmother's roots were Irish—the smiling side of the family.

Like a sneaky cat, the wind cranked up at night, banging limbs of a pine tree across the stucco house and roof. Usually, the wind dies down at night, but was on the prowl this time. The day of cleaning out the house brought dreams and unsettled ghosts. He woke to a rhythmic chirp, to the question of whether the house itself was awake in protest. But it was only the battery run down on a smoke detector, a sign it was time for a new one. In his dream, his wife Claire was in the home. He ran into her in the hall, disoriented. He wanted to ask her what happened, what's going on, but they couldn't speak; they just stood there looking at each other in confusion. They'd spent decades visiting the home when their two children were growing up, exploring the treasures. He took a moment to look at the curious organization of tools in the garage, the familiar games in the family room; one called *Life,* another called *Sorry.*

It's well known, but rarely discussed, that the Santa Ana winds bring more deliriums than dreams. In the next one he was driving and came upon the scene of a car wreck. Young men had gotten out of the car and were standing around. Some were wounded. He ran for help, up a road, to a house with a light on. Someone started to turn a doorknob. He woke to the sound of a garbage truck, with its huge mechanical arm descending to the street, reaching for the can that he'd filled to the top. Everything was emptied. Pierce felt relief, even though the garbage can was immediately toppled by the wind. The thing tumbled thirty feet before catching on a curb.

The morning air was viciously dry and hot by 8:00 A.M. He showered to avoid giving in. Besides, dreams are fickle, always dissolving into the day, demanding your attention, deserting you, shredding the important details. As a psychologist, Pierce found a way of listening to dreams as landscapes where he tried to get close to the dreamer. Try all you want, but you can only hear another person's dreams through your own associations. It's wrong to think of a singular meaning. Some are condensed to a Chinese puzzle. Others are as obvious as a neon sign. Don't forget to look at the objects in the background.

Coming down the hallway, looking for his keys, Pierce remembered telling Morissy something in supervision. "You know I've always had it in the back of my mind that one of our occupational hazards is that of being murdered, probably not by a patient, but by someone who's threatened by the patient getting better. I've even dreamt of it."

"God knows getting better can be dangerous," said Morissy, "in all kinds of ways. Everything is re-considered, marriages and careers. Of course, you can forget tidy endings for the most part. It's part of the territory. Some folks will stay for the longest time and we can't figure why. With others, we wonder what has blunted the edge of need, and what we've accomplished or witnessed. The good-enough therapist can be wildly off the mark. We're no good at all if we don't wonder from time to time about what we're missing, or if we've settled prematurely on a false assumption, but cling to it anyway."

The dry wind romped through the morning and Pierce needed a break from his chores. He headed to downtown Santa Ana, to Broadway, to the *Gypsy Den Cafe,* for delicious eggs and bread, fresh juice and coffee. When he passed the corner of Sycamore and Civic Center Drive, a piece of blue sky emerged from the dust and a group of screaming parrots flew from one palm tree to another. The bells of a church rang out. He settled in, opened his computer, and there was a message from his partner, René, who was taking his mail and checking his calls while he was away.

"All is quiet on the western front. Nothing urgent. Your mystery caller is still at it. No message left, but a longer than usual pause. I thought you'd want to know. Your patient, V, called me with a panic attack and a nightmare that you'd been in a car accident. She wanted to hear your voice through mine. She knows she can call you directly if needed, but she was fine when she spoke with me. It was like the time you were in Italy and she dreamt your plane had crashed. Good thing it wasn't a premonition. By the way, I just had a dream where you brought me a bottle of fine limoncello. I hope it comes true! Miss you!"

After breakfast, a stroll down Fourth Street in Santa Ana saves you a hundred mile drive to the border of Mexico. Window-shopping is a trip in itself; a sea of white in bridal shops, stores with cool boots, advertisements for quinceañeras, food kiosks too. Pierce wondered if Morissy had tried working these streets as Javier. He was fluent in Spanish and he might make friends with the men selling Churros. If you come on Sunday after church, families are dressed up, strolling and shopping, breathing life to the core of the city that was horribly run down when Pierce was growing up. It was heartening; the way that murals on nearby buildings told stories of the culture, but what warmed him most was the way children hold their sibling's hands and actually listen to parents. It's the opposite of all the frowning faces in the upscale shopping centers of Costa Mesa and Newport Beach. All the Escalades and Lexus cars in the world don't translate to the sense of *familia* that you see everywhere in Santa Ana. There's nobody to impress on Fourth Street. A few miles away, there are car dealerships in Newport Beach that make you think of the fall of Rome, but here, in Santa Ana's Birch Park, there are modest paths and intimate shaded spots with plain tables designed for seniors and children. Nobody's in a hurry. Men sit in conversation, playing cards, leaning toward each other; their voices drift past trees and back along the empty places, where grass is free of trash. There is poverty and there is pride. Blue lamp-posts keep vigil and benches face an enigmatic sculpture of a metal sphere representing the world. Pierce had a different take; that he was looking out from the inside of a marble. It made him dwell on the theme of becoming.

In the homeless hub near Civic Center, the theme is bare survival. There's a crush of want and need. You see it in vignettes; a child wearing rags runs to meet her grandfather who sits on a plastic box. He strokes the top of her head; *hola preciosa* is overheard. She sits next to him, settles in and closes her eyes. They have nothing but each other. Nearby, the old courthouse sits like a fortress, with its sculpted anchor bricks as big as small cars. The building is ringed by magnolia trees, 50-foot palms, and shrubs with rounded edges. Across the street, all is white at the First Presbyterian Church.

When he drove by Santa Ana Senior High School, his alma mater was shining with pride. He took a good look at his hands on the steering wheel, the same hands that opened these stately doors. The goodness of youth was there. You can't go back and you can't go forward, you're always in the now. Some magnetic force brought him back to Fourth Street, to see the classic Yost Theatre, renovated, set off from traffic. An art district has sprung up, along with the realities of gen-trification. Thousands of new condos made Pierce cringe. His hometown wasn't vertical back then. He paused to watch a street-style soccer game in a concrete park, with music on loudspeakers and men whistling and shouting, leaning on plywood walls.

The game was serious, aggressive, not for children, all about skill and deception. Over on North Minter, St. Joseph's Church was going strong. Pierce remembered services there with his Catholic grandmother, when Mass was spoken in Latin. He could almost smell the incense and feel the walls that muffled every word. He could hear the repetitive chants, and travel the odd path of his seven-year-old mind in obligatory prayer, knees on wood, unsure what any of it meant. Confusing to a lad, that in his memories, he couldn't remember anyone smiling. Everything was solemn. Shouldn't you be happier if you're going to heaven? If he made the slightest sound, someone turned around to scowl. He heard that Mass was now in Spanish, and relevance had returned.

Only a mile away, on the other side of Seventeenth Street, there's another culture, the elegance of another time on the beautifully manicured, classical homes along streets named Heliotrope and Victoria. The neighborhood of Floral Gardens is filled with the scent of plumeria and elegant cactus gardens. Hibiscus and gardenias are everywhere, along with colors of bougainvillea you've never seen before. Arches and windows are adorned with geraniums and climbing roses. The city was thriving again.

Chapter 15

NIGHT RACE

In the glow of evening, Pierce got an urge to go out to Los Alamitos Racetrack to bet on the quarter horses. Most of the races are over in less than twenty seconds of raw speed, so you don't want to blink. Tails are flying in a display of incredible power. Come to the fence and you'll feel the rush, the thunder of beasts full out, with sod kicked up all around. Something's primal about a night race.

He rushed his bet on the third race, which he lost, owing to some difficulty establishing a link with his mother's method of betting. Funny how you can be a student of sensible betting, and still end up betting on a horse that's gray with a name that reminds you of a high school sweetheart. The problem, of course, is when the hunch pays off, you think you've tapped into a crystal ball and deserve a moment of pure self-admiration. But when you're wrong, you feel stupid, wishing you'd bet on the favorite who only paid three dollars for your two-dollar bet. At least you've won. Coming back time after time is the interesting part, a vacation from decisions that have serious consequences. Hunches are played in therapy too; something motivates you to ask for details here, but not there. A story is told that comes in too neat a package, so it makes you wonder about the aftermath or the part not mentioned. You ask, or your posture does it for you. Suddenly, the hunch pays off and a forbidden memory crashes through the canyons. A piece of personal fiction is dismantled. Another image comes forth—one that's a little more honest. You don't know how it fits with the other parts, you only know it's important. Continuity is challenged as the self expands. You either take it in or try to crush the knowing.

Looking up from his racing form, Pierce made out the outline of someone he thought he'd known in high school. The tall man had a familiar way of tapping his leg with his right hand, glasses an inch down the nose, deep in a study of the changing odds. A trumpeter in a red coat played the fanfare, signaling ten minutes to post time, but the tall man didn't look up from his racing form to see the horses coming onto the track. When he did look up, he walked over with surprising briskness and certainty.

"Hatley Pierce, is that you? I can't believe it, where did the decades go?"

"Everly Tompkins, I presume. My God you look the same. What a trip, I remember you well from high school. I always admired your optimism and how you came out of nowhere to be class president. Look at us now, here at the track, trying to beat the system. I remember you were headed for Caltech, voted the most likely person to be a millionaire by the age of thirty."

"Oh that, well, I was actually a millionaire by twenty-five, but nobody could have predicted the rest. I started a software company, sold it, made a bundle, did it all again, even bought a fifty-foot yacht in Newport Harbor. I used to cruise down to Ensenada all the time, just for kicks. Great Gatsby lifestyle, overrated I can tell you. You can't believe the human leeches you attract when you have money and give parties. I lost it all on the options market, you remember the tech crash? For a while I thought I was a king, got into cocaine, the whole bit. Now I live in a mobile home trying to figure my next move. Keeping it simple suits me. My wife disappeared when the money disappeared. Funny thing about that. I figure I'm better off without her if she was going to whine about a little misfortune. We lost our second home in Carmel, too. Damn, that's the one I miss. At least my kids still love me. Things aren't so bad, I have running water and I'm sweet on a gal who works at a bookstore. She doesn't need me to be a big shot."

Everly pointed to the floor near the betting machines. Hundreds of identical betting tickets were strewn on the ground like an abstract painting. There's tradition to losing, a personal style too. Most people utter a single swear word and flick the losing ticket away, like a bee landed on their hand. Nobody wants to hold a losing ticket. Besides being worthless, it's bad luck. It helps to look at it like the distant past and to get on with the next race. Creative folks bring a touch of drama and throw them over a shoulder, easy come easy go, or just let them drop, like water slipping between the fingers. Angry ones throw the ticket on the floor, but the air catches it and makes it flip or sail for a half a second, as if to mock the holder. A lot of people just sigh. It's intensely private for some, a public display for others. The failure to use a trashcan is a study in itself. Winning tickets go in the shirt pocket or a purse, patted like puppies for security. Everyone has a ritual. It was simply Pierce's nature to notice, not that he had a place to file what he saw.

Everly looked intently at the moths circling the lights above the pretty track, wondering if the bats were feasting.

"I'll recover somehow. I come here to think things over, here in the company of losers. I'm a sucker for the ponies. What can I say? When I was rich, I'd go to Del Mar, Hollywood Park, Santa Anita for the thoroughbreds. A touch of elegance never hurt a guy. But here's where the regular people go. Gritty, the place and the patrons could use a good wash down, but here we are. I still think something good will happen in my life. Listen, do you have an extra fifty bucks? I'm fresh broke after that last cheating scum of a jockey held my horse back. I'm sure he got paid off. Crooked business, I swear, but some of these races aren't fixed, and just now I got a phone call from beyond. I'm telling you, old friend, the nine horse is going to win, and she's coming to the gate at twenty-five-to-one."

"How do you figure?" Asked Pierce, curious but cautious.

"She's coming down in class, has been miserable for the last five races, but look, back in January she came from behind to win, and won easily, look at her time, almost a track record. She has it in her and her time is due; I can feel it. What say you? If we win, we'll split it, and if not, we've still won, since what are the odds of running into an old friend in a place like this?"

"You know," Pierce said, "my mother said that numerology is for real, that sometimes numbers line up in patterns and it's not a coincidence. She used the date plus the jockey's last name, the pole position, the name of the trainer, and threw in a bunch of other variables she thought were relevant. A long name becomes a single number. It all reduces to a pattern of numbers, like three nines for the ninth race, meaning the cosmic forces are coming together. She used to circle the patterns with a thin red pen."

Pierce studied the racing form intently, trying to remember the variables she used. For a solid minute he turned into a scholar in an ancient library. "Wow, look at this," he said, "nines are coming up strong, practically screaming at us. You're on."

At the betting machine, Pierce got the ticket and even tripled his bet on a horse named Athena's Muse. For a little insurance, he bet her across the board, to win, place, and show, and wheeled her up and down in the exacta for extra measure. He figured that if he was wrong, it's no big deal; you can chalk it up to cosmic interference in the space-time continuum. Mortals can't be expected to figure out the future. You have to forgive yourself for missing a weather forecast, why not this?

One bonus is you get to see the unique way everyone has of holding a ticket that will either become trash or cash in the next few minutes. That's the interesting part. They went down to the fence near the finishing line where you can smell the turf and hope for a photo finish.

"What about you? Asked Everly. You were a photographer for the high school yearbook, always chronicling everything, trying to capture moments."

"I ended up studying biology and psychology but the future didn't declare itself to me in college. I barely missed a trip to Vietnam, moved to San Francisco and then hitchhiked across the country. I should have died getting into cars with psychopaths, jumping on freight trains too. Of course, there were strange liaisons with women, a few hallucinogens in unlikely places. I damaged my ears at concerts, stupidly getting right up to the speakers for The Doors, The Cream, Janis Joplin, The Grateful Dead, and twenty other bands. Hitched across Europe and nearly died in the Moroccan desert from dysentery. You know, the usual story of our generation. A little protesting, but mostly confusion.

"Remember our English teacher, Mr. Crispin?" asked Everly. "Man, that guy predicted each of us was going to act out a variation of a character from a Greek or Roman myth, and he said it was a crying shame that we weren't mature enough to see our own stories were already forming. He leaned on the edge of his desk and invited us to come to the party. At least you and I were listening. Remember how we looked at each other across the room, like a candle was lit. The man was right all along."

"Yeah, who would have thought I'd be a clinical psychologist? Not that a psychologist cures anything, just that it's as real as I can handle. Before graduate school I was smitten with my wife in a darkroom romance. Now I have a nice home near a river, children with Shakespearean qualities I'll never come close to figuring out. I never made much money, so I never tested the theory that money ruins things."

"You, a psychologist? Come on! You're joking or you're lying. Which is it? You're too restless. I never imagined you being able to sit still for more than five minutes. I figured you for a documentary photographer. I saw a therapist once. She told me I've got a serious problem, that I'm quite the dreamer, that it was a good thing I tilt toward optimism, because I'd be crushed by my own depressions otherwise. She said I had Bipolar Disorder, that it accounted for my genius moments, my grandiosity, also my impulsive disasters, like going days without sleep, inventing languages I didn't understand, getting secret messages in television commercials. It was weirder than hell to be told that the only me I know is actually a disorder. Would I trade myself in for a conventional life? Hell no. Anyway, my therapist kept checking off symptoms on a piece of paper. I didn't like her but I have to admit the medications saved me more than once, but for the love of God, who invented the idea that the goal of life should be stability? What about art? What about passion? Oh yeah, I did try to kill myself a few times when I lost all the money, but look, the gulls are circling low to the ground in the middle of the track. It means the Santa Ana winds are done blowing. The night air is getting dense, you can feel it. The fog is forming. It means something unexpected is going to happen."

"Everly, with your smarts, you could write software in your sleep, keep a low profile, get back on your feet financially, then figure your next move. The last reunion of our high school class was fun, but I didn't see you there. Fortunately we had big nametags so you didn't have to guess the names. You know, I've always believed that half of what makes anyone interesting is what they do when they're in some kind of trouble or reverie, but I'm glad you got the care when you needed it. The Bipolar thing is real, that much I can tell you. Let's see who's going to win this race?"

Privately, Pierce couldn't help contrasting Everly with Morissy, who wouldn't allow his despair to be seen by others and had to submerge the shame that his soul was bleeding. Everly put it all right out there. Pierce wondered how to figure the odds of these two men surfacing? One an open book, the other in disguise.

Then came the announcement over the loudspeaker, "Aaaaand they're off!" The race itself was a blur. The announcer called it, but nobody listened. You have to watch a race your own way. From a distance their hopes took a beating, as *Athena's Muse* went out of the gate far wide, usually the kiss of death. *Charlie's Parade* stumbled and bumped lightly into *Allegra,* but not so hard as to warrant an infraction. The game was on and the favorite, *Three Wishes,* blew by the rest of the field, leaving *Willow Glen* and *Believer* eating dust. When *Desperado* came between horses near the rail, there seemed no other fate, but she fell back just as quickly. *Princessa's Joy* and *Fable Monkey* were never really in the race, which was coming to the wire. The full-on sprint was furious to behold, and from the outer reaches came *Athena's Muse,* surprising the favorite, who couldn't see her coming on. The jockey held up a hand in victory, surprised at having won. *Athena's Muse* was a stunner in the winning circle, black and steaming under the glaring lights, full of race and grace, even when it was over. Pierce and Everly were full of high-fives, with well over a thousand dollars to share. Pierce was generous, and shared his exacta winnings too.

"Oh, man, you and your phone call!" Pierce cried out, smiling ear to ear.

"Your numerology thing didn't hurt either, so back at ya," said Everly. "I'm going to buy my new gal a pretty dress, maybe parlay this into a thousands more and buy a better car. I'm calling this night a turning point. I'm very glad you showed up."

"I'm quitting for the night. I hate the feeling of losing my handle right after winning. I've done that so many times I ran out of places on my body to kick myself. Good luck, my friend."

The two said something about the fates bringing them to the track on a future night, but they didn't exchange information. The effect was like visiting a distant cousin you'll probably never see again; not sadness, just a glimpse of an old friend in an intersection. Still, the evening penetrated, stirring other embers. On the way home, Pierce had a close call in the parking lot. Someone was drunk, screeching to get out, speeding like a maniac where people were walking to their cars. It was a woman who shouldn't have come to the track at all, angry at the world. Probably she'd gambled away her paycheck. The old sad story, for which Pierce was almost collateral damage.

Chapter 16

MORNING AT SHAW'S COVE

Pierce gave himself two-to-one odds that Morissy would beg off another meeting, bracing himself for a disappearance. But you shouldn't bet against hope when your reasons are made of mud. It's good to be wrong sometimes. He spotted Morissy coming down the stairs like he had a special purpose.

Some will say that Shaw's cove in North Laguna is best visited in late afternoon for the stunning play of light. But on any foggy morning, the echoes of your thoughts are so close, you can't ignore their calls. It's a good thing the Keeper of Shaw's Cove is with you, guardian of introspection. She's always nearby, whether you seek her out or don't. Pierce invented her a long time ago as a fable, a way of explaining the visitations that came to him at Shaw's Cove. Most were completely unexpected, and he left it to The Keeper to decide who would visit from his past.

The beach itself is another crescent, with flat rock formations in the center and on the ends. The cliffs don't bruise your eyes with someone's conspicuous wealth. Up top, there's a small gazebo and a cluster of palms. Below, readers and thinkers sit close to the bluffs among the larger pieces of driftwood. Over the years, Pierce was struck by how many people gravitate here for solitude. More often than not, someone would crouch at water's edge and scoop a handful of sand, making it their whole world. Today was more for walking.

A Japanese woman rocked back and forth from her crouch as if she wanted to cry but couldn't. Everyone gave her plenty of room to converse with the ocean, which must have answered, since she moved on by the time Pierce and Morissy greeted each other. Pierce was still meditating on the stillness of her crouch and the tangle of black hair that covered half her face.

Finally, Pierce spoke to his friend. "As you can see, I'm in love with Shaw's Cove. It's my favorite place for contemplation. Everything I think about goes straight out to sea as a kind of offering, or bounces off the bluff. Either way, a response comes back in waves and whispers. I'm delivered from half my worries. I can't say what forces are here, but if I'm alone for just a few minutes, I find a little peace, a place where things are seen without asking."

Morissy nodded as if he felt the same and was determined to see for himself. He must have had a swim in mind since he wore a bathing suit under his clothes, which he left in a lump on the sand. He went into the water without the usual pause to take stock of the cold. When he was waist deep, he stopped to look at the horizon, like he was re-thinking the idea of immersion. A few waves knocked him back, but he steadied himself each time, defying his own physical frailty; *too thin for his own good,* thought Pierce. Then his friend dove in and disappeared, taking long breast strokes underwater, surfacing at the edge of Pierce's worry, to swim twenty strokes before heading back for shore.

He was triumphant coming out of the water, found his towel, dried his face, and draped it around his shoulders. "It's coming back to me. I've been here before, a long time ago, but I never got in the water. I need the ocean more than I thought."

Pierce quipped something about the ocean calling, but it didn't make sense to think the ocean needs anything from humans. Besides, it was terrible timing. You shouldn't speak right when a person has more to say.

They settled on silence in the meantime, walking the length of the beach. On their way back, Pierce announced it was an irony that he gave the fictional name Eve to his fourth patient on Tuesdays.

"I could have called her Tuesday Morningside, or some variation, but I didn't. What's in a name? I've been seeing her twice a week for six months. When I'm with her, as with this beach, my thoughts come back to me distilled, smoothed over, slightly out of reach. That's it! I'm troubled by whether she's really calm or just terribly surrendered."

Morissy looked at a young boy exploring the creatures in a tide pool.

"There's a gigantic difference between the narrative the patient delivers and the story you create." Morissy picked up a small round rock and tossed it in the brine. "You know, there was a time when I might have asked you why you invented the name Eve to guard your patient's privacy, and also why you give feminine qualities to this beach, but I've come to trust the need to give it a rest, to appreciate the art of a person, which is so much more than the sum of the parts they tell. We find pieces of ourselves sooner or later when we try to describe others. It's always a bit unnerving."

"You know me well, how I can't stop wondering if something is symbolic and whether I should chase it or leave it alone. Usually, I come here in the evening. I suppose that explains the name Eve. As for the feminine quality, it's just the way the cove holds me, nothing more to say. Here's the thing; Eve is eager to talk. She bounces her insights off the outer edge of me, but interrupts me if I start to respond. She has soliloquies that go in circles, like she's trying to convince herself that her malaise is lifting, but everything about her presence says otherwise. Soon the hour is at an end.

"She reassures me again and again that she's fine, but I sense her foundation is cracking. People have written about sham insight and who am I to judge? It's like she's doing self-analysis in front of me and I'm held to witness the way she diminishes herself with explanations. Remember the way a vinyl record can get stuck in a groove and play the same bit over and over? I know I can't just move the needle. I'm looking more carefully into how I'm stuck in my own way of listening. All the while, something knocks on the doors of recognition.

Here's a recent development; she's starting to accept I'm an actual person in the other chair. She's noticing my mood and gestures, beginning to ask questions. There's a more fluid exchange. Change is coming, I'm not sure which kind."

Morissy stopped rather abruptly and it wasn't something Pierce had said. A large group of sandpipers held court on the sand directly in their path. They turned into a fine gray cloud when they flew out over the water.

"Sorry," he said, "please go on. I always stop for birds."

"Her fiancé was killed in a car wreck six months before I saw her, yet she had a strange sense of relief. She never told a soul that the relationship wasn't going well, and she's not even sure that's how she was feeling. The idea came to her like a starfish she hadn't seen before, one that blends with the rocks in a tide pool. She mentioned it in speculation. I have the odd sensation Eve needs me to listen for the parts she can't tell. Really, it's an honored role. So far, she hasn't been able assign meaning in the loss of her fiancé. I had a vision during a recent session; I'm in a hospital emergency room and a curtain is drawn across one of the cubicles. There's a small gap I can see through. Eve is the patient, telling an unseen person she's devastated, that she exists in a disembodied state. Something was stolen from her and she's not sure what it was. Everything is terribly wrong and now her only safety is to live by a set of rules. She must pretend to be neutral, with no desire for a relationship, or to change jobs, move, travel, or even try a new restaurant. She's only thirty-seven, physically very healthy. She says her friends are *really nice,* with no elaboration."

Inexplicably, Morissy started walking backward, but kept his pace with Pierce.

"I do this from time to time. I either walk backward or think backward. I think you're actually describing yourself as much as you're describing her. I also think she's grieving another, earlier loss, maybe several, but doesn't know it. Of course, it's just a hunch. What does an old man know? We try to work with people where we find them, not where they would like to be, or more to the point, we shouldn't rush to identify a central problem, like I just did. Maybe we can't help it and we need these transitional ideas more than we admit. But they're too much like abbreviations of a person. It's not easy to remain mindful in spite of the lofty goal. You say in your vision she's declared that nothing new can come into her life, yet there you are, a new person, when it's forbidden. This brings risk for her. I hope you pay keen attention in your glances through the curtain. It's a wild thought, but what if she's trying to speak to you from behind your own curtain? What else is going on?"

"Toward the end of our last session, she looked right at me, which was very different than her usual fussing with her purse and coat. She told me that during the past year, while driving home from work, she'd been listening to a particular portion of Bach's *Mass in B Minor* on a CD, until one day the CD warped and became unplayable. That's when she called for therapy—when she couldn't play that exact piece on her treasured CD. She could have just bought another copy, or downloaded it from the Internet, but she called me instead."

"Dear lad, this is the finest introduction that you've given me in, well, ever! She's starting to let you contain her unformulated regions, and you're trying to make it safe enough for her to begin to hear herself. It comes in flashes, yours and hers; that's how you'll know of movement. Your instincts are good. It would be easy to label her problems, but it would be a tragedy. Don't distance yourself from her subjective world, from her need to be the way she is at the moment. It would be like telling her she's painting a portrait of a sunset just because she put a yellow dot on the canvas. To appreciate her, you must engage in the deepest listening you can bear. Don't try to push the river or go after defenses head on, or some similar nonsense they used to teach us, you know, to get at the so-called underlying affect. Traumatic things need special attention since the body reacts before the mind remembers. Some evening when you come here alone, she might speak to you from the bluffs and tell you she's afraid that you'll give her some all-encompassing summary tied up in a tidy bow, and then push her out the door. You have to be wary of that script."

"It's odd," replied Pierce, bending to pick up the skeleton of a sea urchin, known in the biology world as a *test*. "I have a mirror image of that same thought, that someday, any day, with a swish of her long silk scarf, she'll announce that she's grateful for the work, for my time and kindness, and doesn't need to come anymore."

"She might, but I think you're both carriers of this interesting fear and might be able to talk about it directly if she stays. By the way, I went through a period of listening to Mozart's *Requiem* every day for a long time and never told anyone until this very moment. I suppose it was some combination of melancholy and beauty that expressed a feeling I guarded, but it allowed me a kind of profound and private recognition. The last thing I wanted was to figure it out. I never wanted the *Requiem* to be for me. It wasn't that simple. I wanted to be swept into it, to be carried. That's what I remember. The need finally played itself out. There comes a time when our patients don't want to hear our ideas, our theories, at all. They want our way of paying attention, of being present."

"It's true," said Pierce. "I supervise new therapists and they're super prone to worrying if therapy is too smooth or too dramatic, too confrontational, too erotic, too deflected with humor, and so on. It's hard for anyone to get better with all this worrying going on. I remember you showing me an academic paper you wrote on exactly this topic and no journal would publish it. I think it was one of your best."

"I remember. It touched on the personal worries of the therapist getting activated within the stories they hear. Editors didn't want to get into it back then—the old argument about whether we're forcing the patient to fit into our model of the mind or burdening the patient with our personal associations. As if it had to be one or the other. With all this talk of burdening, I was trying to explore the conversations that flow beyond the words we say, not an imposition of will."

Morissy kicked a hole in the sand as if to bury some memories. "You know, I loved most of my colleagues. I never really thought I had a better way."

He became animated and turned to walk forward again. "Now that I've gone around the bend, I suppose I can chalk it up to the Keeper of Shaw's Cove. I always found it incredible how the sameness of a therapy room can be like a launching pad or a landing strip. We don't know at first. The natural world lives in us all. I loved it when patients made repeated references to a particular place: a forest, a lake, a desert, or what it's like on Mars. Their places acquired a mysterious validity, a place where things could be felt in honesty. Think about it, the mention of a place can function as a kind of hypnotic induction, a refuge, an invitation. I was developing ideas for working with those with painful attachment histories. I miss this work immensely."

"Good thing you have Mozart and I have these beaches inside of me. I'm listening to Corelli and Tomaso Albinoni these days. I suppose I need the structures, the textures in my life right now. Soon enough I'll go back to the blues, maybe some country rock or Mexican pop." Pierce picked up a broken clam and felt the smoothness of the inner part. Morissy picked up a handful of sand and made a little hourglass, letting a thin stream flow out the bottom.

Two pelicans flew over them to mark the moment, close enough so the men could hear their wings beating the air. Pierce was visited by the memory of a different patient, Natalie, whom he saw at the very beginning of his training. He didn't mention it to Morissy. He remembered the moment she first cried, a tear falling on her leg, saying something he thought he'd never hear.

"I'm crying because I'm too normal. I have no great loss, no interests you could even call hobbies, no sense of passion, and no feeling that unbalances me. I can't imagine being special to anyone. Look how bad this is. I'm not even sure it's a good thing to be special to someone. Relationships might be a disappointment. Why take a chance?"

The year before, Natalie had taken the Minnesota Multiphasic Personality Inventory in a university clinic and was one of those people with an absolutely normal profile. An intern was happy to report the results—that she had no obvious mood problem, no anxiety to speak of, no impulse problem, no histrionic tendency, no paranoia, was not particularly introverted or extroverted, etc., but she was devastated. The intern thought she would be delighted, and remembered telling Pierce what she said.

"Can't I have a little weirdness that becomes the source of art? I have no desire to create. Who wants to know a person with a flat profile? I sure don't." She found herself at Pierce's door for therapy and he never brought the case to supervision. He never figured out why, only that he needed to go it alone with Natalie.

Morissy had wandered off to inspect a piece of driftwood as large as a person, sculpted by the elements with nubs that looked like limbs. Pierce kept remembering Natalie, who declared her life to be a flat line, no beating heart. She had a crummy job even though she did well in college. She had roommates she rarely saw. He remembered wondering if it was a trap, drawing him in only to enact rejection, confirming her sad belief. All this normality business haunted him. She was beyond complicated as he swam against her tide.

At Shaw's cove, you don't need to ask why someone visits. Natalie appeared by his side, now in her fifties, and smiled the half-hearted way he remembered. In the imagination, anything can happen. It felt natural to put his arm around her shoulder for a walk while Morissy studied his driftwood using both of his weathered hands. She put her arm around Pierce's waist. Everything was simple, wordless. He led her to the edge of water and held her shoes while she danced in the waves like a child. It was an offer late in coming, a restorative fantasy. Nothing in their earlier encounters ever felt so simple.

In the visitation, he flashed on his three years with her, on his refusal to find her dull. She fought him. He fought back. They found themselves in a ballet of push and pull. He'd drift and she'd come find him, restoring him, maddening him by refusing to be interested in the therapist in him. He was rattled since she was often right. In time, she found the version of him she needed. They stumbled through incomplete sentences even when walls were collapsing. There were months when objects had no colors, even his favorite blue vase turned dull. He dreamt of a burning city while she dreamt of being wrapped in a blanket. She developed hobbies, becoming a master of calligraphy, writing prose imitating letters from Elizabethan times. They were beautiful. She was never a flat line again. The business of therapy is not for surface dwellers.

Chapter 17

BREATHING UNDERWATER

Divers come to Shaw's Cove on calm days when it's safe for a beach entry. Clusters of underwater rocks are only a short way out. Pierce started diving here when he was sixteen, when there were still a few red abalones among the green ones. Lobsters too, and scallops. When he first took up scuba diving, the sound of his own breath was a conversation with anxiety. There's a portion of you that stays in disbelief until you learn to trust the equipment. Then you can focus on the world you're visiting. You're not always a welcome guest. The vicious face of a moray eel warns you to keep your distance. The spines of purple urchins are certainly not your friends; neither are sculpin or stingrays. Once, while diving in the kelp forests off Catalina Island, he crossed the path of a placid giant grouper. It was a gentle mystical encounter. The other divers were out of sight. It was intensely private, a boy and a giant fish, motionless for a cosmic minute. There and gone. He remembered the mouth and gills, the other way of breathing.

Morissy returned from his driftwood sculpture and drew a circle in the wet sand with his toe. He added eyes, nose and a mouth with a confusing squiggle.

"I've been out of the therapy world a long time, but I still read journals. Tell me, why do West Coast therapists have to use the word *new* so much in their articles? Have they no humility, no respect for history?" Then, in a quirk of his character, he answered his own question. "I suppose it's envy, the fact that East Coast therapists take off the entire month of August for some serious reprieve. Besides, who wants to be in the city when it's that humid? It's not easy keeping one foot in orthodoxy and the other in revolution. Without August, our workaholic souls would never mend. Blessing or curse, I'm not sure. I miss the cycles of the work, especially the first hint of fall."

Pierce was delighted to engage in lightness, and took the bait to play. "Wow, that piece of driftwood really spoke to you. Mend, you say? So it's true, you never learned the Zen of body surfing. How terribly sad. You're right about the August envy. Out here we think a week off is enough. Who do we think we're kidding?"

"I suppose it is enough if you declare it so," replied Morissy, "but it's almost as sad as a good portion of the art in Laguna Beach. Don't get me wrong, there's great talent here. I've got to say the Pageant of the Masters sounds silly until you see how incredibly well it's done; humans set in frames or posed as statues. It's brilliant, unexpected. But in some of the galleries, why use gloss on wood and garish blue for sky when you have the real thing all around? It's not just Laguna. I've seen the intricate grain in a redwood table absolutely ruined by making it look like plastic. Too many galleries feature paintings that hurt the eyes with obligatory seagulls, sunsets way too orange, that sort of thing. I've got to admit, the sculpture is very original. Explain that to me, no don't. I've been to Carmel too. Mixed blessing. I used to escape to the Marine Room when I first moved here, for a beer and some rock and roll. I miss the Sunday concerts when the Missiles of October were still around. My kind of kick-ass band."

"Now you're speaking my language, my friend, it's a wonder I didn't see you there before, or if I did, the fates weren't ready for us to meet. You go a few miles inland and you're hard pressed to find anything but strip malls and shopping centers. At least there are some hiking trails. If you go south along the coast, the *Chart House* overlooks Dana Harbor. There's a euro lounge feel at the bar and a pretty lawn that overlooks the harbor. I used to work at Dana Point with the Harbor Patrol as a lifeguard when the boat slips were being constructed.

The jetty was already in. It was devastating knowing it would never be natural again. At least the blue whales come back frequently in summer, just a few miles offshore. The Tall Ships Festival is worth the wait, and the Ocean Institute is a little gem, not to mention the beach at the tip of Dana Point. You should go out whale watching when the bottlenose dolphins are around. They can sense your feelings you know. They look right into you before diving under the boat. You won't forget their eyes. The common dolphins are playful too, sometimes in the hundreds."

Chapter 18

A FAR CRY FROM NORMAL

Coming up the stairs from Shaw's Cove, Morissy mumbled something about the novels *Moby Dick,* and *The Old Man and the Sea,* some linking theme, but he seemed to be speaking to himself. Pierce dropped back a few steps and recalled their goofy moments from long ago. They amounted to a small collusion to challenge the pitfalls of self-importance while admitting it's not so easy. You could call it a contradiction but it was closer to a paradox. During supervision meetings, Morissy would stop what he was saying, back up, and go down another street in his mind. Pierce would follow as far as he could, or was allowed. Both would milk the waters of mock guilt when, for any reason, circumstances disrupted their meetings. One of them would invariably claim dramatic illness in an e-mail or phone message. "I would love to see you today, but I've been vomiting."

It became outrageous. Pierce might find himself responding, "Gosh, I'm sorry, I've been vomiting too, plus I have a relapse of Dengue Fever, but I'd still like to meet with you if you're up for it." Then Morissy would cook up something like, "You really wouldn't want to see me like this, all soiled and disheveled. My patient threw a cup of water at me. I deserved it. I blew the session and can't offer you anything today. Seriously, I'm sorry to cancel, see you next week."

A normal man would have let it go, but Pierce upped the ante, saying, "Even your depleted self would be valuable if you still want to meet. Don't worry about little old me. I'll be fine, but my patients will suffer horribly."

Morissy was a far cry from normal also, and might say, "Good one, Dr. Pierce, crude, but well played. I've taught you well, but I have no idea what I've taught. Now I'm physically

sick plus I'm worried about your lack of independent func-
tioning. Anyway, next week is good." When they would
eventually meet, there was never a mention of the exchange.

In time, Pierce learned two sides of his mentor: the formal
and the enigmatic interior. Every minor aspect of a case was
open to exploration. But something had caused a dark turn,
and Pierce began to wonder if Morissy had a patient who had
threatened him for real. It occurred to him there was some
trouble he wasn't allowed to know, and it bothered him. After
all, not much had been said about the loss of Morissy's wife,
his physical health, or his drift into serious depression.

Chapter 19

MORISSY ON MORPHINE

Six years ago, Pierce visited Morissy in the hospital when he had to have prostate surgery. Morissy made light of the whole matter, saying he would be taking a few days off for a routine procedure. He had no relatives to visit him, and the way he said the word *routine* dropped off the edge of a cliff. A few colleagues dropped by, and Pierce was among them. June had passed away only months before, and Morissy alluded to a wish for his cancer to take him to his wife. He couldn't bring himself to say that it would have been a solution, but you could tell from his tone. The surgery was more complicated than anticipated. More tissue had to be taken than usual. The doctors didn't smile, even though they thought they got it all. Morphine was on board.

When Pierce visited, Morissy was in brilliant form, playing it straight. He gave Pierce the opportunity to hand him a glass of water that was just out of reach, pretending, inexplicably, to be blind. It was really silly because he had just commented from way across the room on Pierce's bad taste in mixing a burgundy shirt with brown pants, like the image in the doorway was killing him, so he clutched his chest.

"Now you've done it, all my work with you, for nothing! Burgundy simply doesn't go with brown." This was the respect they had for each other. "This mismatch of clothing is just the kind of thing that could finish me off you know." Pierce looked down and realized he'd been given a grand opening, but froze in a mix of relief and worry. Finally, he found a wry smile.

"So you're not blind, thank God! You know, nobody else gives me honest feedback about my dress. My wife has given up. I'm a miserable dresser. Here's your water. I'd put whiskey in it, but I'm hoping the morphine does the trick."

Just as Pierce started to inquire about his friend's health, Morissy blurted out, "Enough about me, tell me about your first patient of the day. I need a good story."

It was absurd to comply with a request to talk about work when his friend was laid up and messed up, but he was relieved that Morissy wanted to engage, so he made up a fictional patient on the spot.

"Ok if you insist."

Even in his narcotic haze, Morissy must have smelled a rat.

"The unconscious is always at work, don't ever forget." But Pierce was undaunted, and brought up the psychotherapy of a man who had received a heart transplant and had a persistent fantasy that he died on the operating table and now demands proof that this life is actually real. Pierce pulled his chair close to the bed so his voice could be heard over the constant beeping of machines.

"My challenge with my patient is that early in therapy, before his heart transplant, we had several discussions about the nature of reality, and sometimes my patient joked that he made me up, and in fact he couldn't be sure that I hadn't made *him* up, and he wondered if he exists only in my mind. How would you suggest I proceed on this matter, Dr. Morissy?" Tongue was firmly in cheek.

"Wait a minute. I'm having the same problem with you, right now! I think I'm alive, talking to you after surgery, but how can I be sure you aren't the angel who's come for me. I'll need reassurance on that point."

Pierce fumbled around for words, and looked steadily at the drips from the IV stand, following the tubes from his friend's arm to the eyes.

"Angels don't wear brown pants, it's forbidden, simply not allowed. You'll have to trust me." Even in his drugged state, Morissy had something to say.

"Ok, you've convinced me for now, but we'll have to revisit this question. Actually, your patient will benefit from simply talking to his new heart in front of you, welcoming it, asking it questions, describing the kind of home the heart will have. You have to give the heart the status of a third presence. We shouldn't underestimate the power of Gestalt therapy. *Of course* we make each other up, some more than others, even at the expense of gaslighting. Did you ever read my famous paper on gaslighting?"

"No, I'm afraid I missed that one. I thought I read everything you wrote."

"Ha, got you! Because I never wrote a paper on gaslighting, although I should have, since it's such a part of human interaction. Little instances of it are far more common than we think, just under the radar of conscious intention. As for me, I've gotten rid of my diseased prostate, and I don't need one to stay alive, so I won't be talking to it. I'm grateful, I think. I'm just hoping I don't need diapers too long and that my dick still works once in a while. How's yours by the way, I mean your prostate? You know my problem was found in a routine screening?" Morissy was loose around the edges, and it was delightful.

"I'm very glad this prostate business isn't going to take you out of action." Just as Pierce was going to get a tiny bit maudlin, Morissy, a master at timing, lifted the arm that did not have an IV in it, and found a perfect response.

"Don't feel sorry for me. At least I'm not drooling. That's always been my big fear, I probably never told you. My big fear as a therapist is that of filling up with confusion right in the middle of a therapy session and to just start drooling; not because of having a stroke, just the end result of accumulated confusion." He mustered a quarter of a smile.

"It's incredible. That's always been one of my fears too," Pierce said, somehow with a straight face. "But what if drooling is what humankind needs to just accept, perhaps more than anything else? It's so honest, so indicative of need and desire. Pavlov's dog heard a bell and in classical conditioning came to associate the bell with food. We have our own interesting associations, desires that function like hunger, fears that we're off the mark, and our reactions are closer to drooling than we care to admit. Nobody writes academic pieces about the relationship between psychotherapy and drooling, or if the Hokey Pokey is what it's all about."

"Not so fast my young doctor. What if silence between people is just a derivative of drooling? What if the Hokey Pokey *is* what its all about?" He grinned hugely, to which there could be no real response other than to laugh nervously at first, then roar so loud the nurse came in. This was the moment when they knew of a certain love between cautious men, which is not so easy to find. "Now that we've cleared that up, continue with your case and leave no detail out."

But Pierce got no further than a few more words when Morissy fell to his much-needed sleep. Just to be sure it was sleep and not some acting job, Pierce said something absurd, that his patient had the most challenging delusion he'd ever heard; that he had turned into the clock that nibbled at the June day in *Mrs. Dalloway,* and somehow he was responsible for the suicide of the incredible author, Virginia Woolf. His patient wondered if the shredding would ever stop.

Pierce remembered the visit like it was yesterday. Time isn't important to the Keeper of Shaw's Cove.

Chapter 20

FISHERMAN'S COVE

At the top of the stairs, Morissy announced he had to take off the rest of the day, but seemed to be rattled, like there was something he didn't want to talk about. He asked if they could meet the next day, at Moss Point Beach in the afternoon. Pierce took to wandering up and down the street that hugs the coves, around and beyond the succulents and rock gardens, the balanced landscapes of beautiful homes. It was years since he'd descended to Fisherman's Cove, a tiny beach with a huge temperament. He likened it to a side chapel of an ancient church in Italy, where the hum of high vespers reaches across the centuries and the walls are slowly crumbling. Everything is close. Even the whispers have echoes.

At Fisherman's Cove, the sand creeps like lava one minute, then back and forth like a metronome. To the open mind on a turbulent day, it's a place you can't easily leave. You can leave in the normal way, but it finds a way to follow. He'd seen people come halfway down the stairs only to turn back, fearing being trapped by a sleeper wave if the tide is high enough. On rough days, it's claustrophobic, too raw and dangerous, but on calm days, if you stay, you'll find a shipwreck of battered presumptions. It's a hard kiss, a feeling that doesn't leave your lips. Stay, if only a few minutes when the surf is rising, and find out what has stirred. No one can say what happens here, it's just that you won't forget.

Pierce wanted the mid-sized waves to wash his thoughts away, and none of his Tuesday patients claimed turf in his mind. It was Morissy he was worried about. He sat in the open, where permanence plays a game with motion. Seaweed comes to shore all shredded, torn by rocks offshore. A man and a woman were fishing from the south rocks; statues with a bucket. They would be perfect in bronze. The man spoke, the woman nodded, and reached for something in their tackle box. If you come on a quiet night under a full moon, the seduction is complete.

Chapter 21

THE POINT OF EVERYTHING

The next morning, Pierce went to the exposed little beach at the foot of Dana Point. Its concentrated energy brings a pinch of anxiety. You have the usual array of choices: look straight out, down to the objects in the sand, straight up, or inward, or any variation. But there's another choice at Dana Point: to look behind you and up. If you lean against the base of the cliff, you'll wonder if today's the day for a slight tremor. Among the other swirling thoughts, you can't shake the thought of an instant end by tumbling rocks.

Up close, a woman works on a project, beading necklaces on a blanket. She sings and you want to hear the words. You see she's calm and wise. A glance away, a couple huddles under a blanket, lost in a kiss. Pierce almost mistook them for boulders. He came alone, when the sea lions were crying. His hands stayed in the bottom of his pockets.

It was a stunning day for sailing. He climbed on a rock to watch a spinnaker go up on a magnificent yacht headed north, then several other sailboats left the harbor, catching the wind with ease. The vista was a portrait in progress.

Between the final brush strokes, he couldn't ignore the thought that Morissy had other secrets. Like his cancer had flared up, or he had to move on, or someone was giving him trouble. He wondered if Morissy had made a monument to his own lamentations and would simply die alone, full of regret. He also wondered if Morissy's faked suicide was designed to flee from someone who had threatened his life or that of his patients. Every wild thought came rushing.

Pierce shifted his gaze to geological history written in layers of the cliff; each has a story, an era, a beginning and an end. Pierce wanted to talk with Morissy about Ava, but realized he couldn't bring her name to him ever again. Plus, he couldn't tell the difference between needing something from his old mentor and needing to make some private peace. He decided on the latter.

For years, he'd been fishing, not the baited kind, not with line and hook, but the wanting kind. He was curious to know more about Ava's years with Morissy, how he'd taken her as a patient right out of the hospital after a serious suicide attempt. She was in and out of hospitals for a few years, and by her own account, a brat one day, indifferent the next, a dreamer all the while. She didn't like the world, or herself in it. Two years ago, she told Pierce she was comfortable to be all-in with him, but it took many full moons before she mentioned she'd actually seen him talking with Morissy at conferences and lectures in the old days, when she had thoughts of being a psychoanalytic historian, never a clinician.

Morissy offered her a few names in case she wanted an independent consultation during a rough spot in her treatment. Pierce's name was among them. She never called. It was a mixed brew trying to imagine how she filed things away, never telling Pierce what the impasse was about. He asked on a single occasion, but she preferred to keep it private. He figured they would have their own troubles someday, and they'd deal with it directly. After all, what good therapy doesn't suffer through a flood or famine or both.

Pierce likened their tension to the stirring of coals beneath ashes. He was drawn to the unexpected things; the weird details about her marriage and her art that hungered for colors in nature. She was not sexy but she was uncannily sexy. She could be abrupt, but it would take a novel to describe it. She had the tiniest of hesitations. When she looked around the room and found him after one of her reveries, her words were a metered sonnet. She rarely needed rage anymore. Once, she wore a coat and took it off her shoulders, just a few inches; the image was pure Ava. Pierce took over her treatment for profound depression shortly after Morissy was memorialized. Both men were drawn to the sensitivity of her privacy, even her darkest doubts.

In one of her first sessions with Pierce, Ava told him, "It's rather simple on one level. I must say this since you never will. Dr. Morissy is gone, now I have you and you have me."

It was a relief she said it exactly that way, with a concreteness he wouldn't have mustered. They spent a year together before he announced he was moving to California. In six months, she took a position as an art historian at a local college and asked to continue in his practice. He wondered if she had followed him, if something ominous was at play. In the end, nothing felt wrong about continuing. Besides, she never played suicide rescue games. Between morbid dreams and childhood things, they planted a redwood forest. In truth it was dance that helped her at least as much as therapy. And art, the great revealer, was often the better language for the all the colliding parts.

He asked the rising wind, *is she my mystery caller?* Part of him was fearful, but the wind said *no*.

Ava appreciated that Pierce wasn't going to pry stories out of her. When she gave him her eyes, she seemed to have no questions, no questions at all, like all she wanted was reassurance that he could see into her without her asking what he saw. She couldn't stand having to give context and it created a feeling that the moment would suffice. She de-constructed the reasoning part of him until all he could see were the tides at Nova Scotia.

One thing Pierce wanted to ask Morissy was what to do with the fact she never liked the exploration of what things mean. Then he remembered how artistic souls like Ava and June are loath to explain their art. Ava could be a lump of wet laundry when she was down, and the next visit, she'd rise like mist from a frozen rooftop in the sun, vanishing in the blue. Never a full mania, always some reserve, always the lovely contradictions. Even when she was a smoldering volcano, she lingered at his door before leaving a session. Not long, just an extra few seconds. She still had thoughts of suicide, but grew beyond the impulse. It was just a fact of her mind that she often thought of dying. She told him more than once, "What's the point of therapy if you can't be honest about what is there?"

He was keen to see where his hands travelled during therapy sessions with Ava. They roamed the space around his body like restless ghosts, unable to settle, as if a house was left abandoned and the ghosts were looking for a place to rest. Ava's hands often stayed in her lap, one covering the other. On a recent evening, her hands broke free and she leaned forward, caressing the sides of her chair as if she would rise. Instead she found her softest voice.

"Sometimes I imagine us not being people at all. It's hard enough caring, anticipating eventual loss. I imagine us more as places for each other, or shape-shifters that transform into animals or landscapes. When I was melting, Dr. Morissy was like ice on a private pond. I could sit at the edge or skate. When I needed to be a bird, I could fly over the surface to the ridge beyond. He was winter, but never a storm. I got to be the storm. We somehow needed it that way. Just now, you are the ocean, a warm ocean I can swim in. Last week you were a cottonwood tree and I was the wind. I'm determined to be a songbird, a viper, a wolf-child, as needed. Isn't that what doctors sometimes prescribe, medications as needed? I'm glad to be an artist. Once, I wanted to be a scholar of the healing arts. I didn't talk about it because I didn't want your opinion. It's not like I'm a great example of healing myself. But I was able to let go of trying to be like the people who helped me. How can you stand trying to be helpful all the time? I've been thinking that our work will soon be done. I'm surprised at stepping into my life, with all my new companions."

Pierce found his own voice, not trying to be like Morissy. "I respect everything you've said. I'm convinced that therapy is less about intentional helping than we know. It's always potent for me, the turn of the page, the moments that defy words. Ava, I trust you're the best judge of what you need and are capable of giving it to yourself. I also trust in your freedom to find your places and forms; it's the work of self, nothing less."

When she began the talk of ending, he thought about Arcangelo Corelli, whether a lost composition would be found in the attic of a tiny European town, companion to rotting wood and the dust of three hundred years? Is there a piece hidden away by a student of the master, a piece that's wild, with no harmonic ending, where violins are stubbornly rising, refusing to come back to earth? Perhaps the piece ends suddenly in the rising, but was never intended to signify death. It's a matter of uneasy contemplation whether care for others can ever be free of self-interest. It was one of the gems uttered by Dr. Morissy to the green and willing Pierce.

Chapter 22

ENCOUNTER AT MOSS POINT

Near the entrance to Moss Beach, there's a house from a childhood dream, with an actual sign on it, labeled, "The Ark," with wonderful curves and arches and a delicious wooden walkway. Someone with huge imagination made it happen. On a calm day, Moss Point Beach sits quietly in the back of your mind. But when the south swell surges, your thoughts are tangled in the hair of a cousin of Medusa. You see it when the swell rises over the rocks and subsides. She's determined to stir you up.

Pierce made up a myth; three sisters were stranded in a shipwreck and died arm-in-arm on the beach. Their ghosts still roam the shallows. If you're drawn to just one of them, the others are jealous and attack. You soon forget about the outer waves because the sisters are closer than you think, in the grass and moss inshore, calling with soft undulations. Their names are Pity, Mercy, and Felicia. They love you if you love them back, and cry if you don't look for them.

Pierce lost track of time and fell asleep against a rock. His psychotherapy patients often told stories as if they called on myths they never knew were theirs. What he thought he was inventing was never his to own.

Before drifting off, he listened to the battle of waves against the outer rocks. The tide would be out for several more hours. The effect was a mournful song. The sharpest rocks are just underwater. Pierce had once seen waves smash into to a thirty-foot cloud that quickly turned to mist. That's where he first saw the faces of the sisters.

A shadow came over him and jogged him awake. It was Morissy, who brought a folding chair and a thermos this time. He jumped right in.

"Sorry to leave suddenly last visit. I had a little matter in court to attend to, an accumulation of unpaid tickets for being an unlicensed popcorn man. I had to pay a big fine. Good thing the judge was old and sympathetic. And a better thing that I bought a bunch of Apple and Google stock a long time ago and cashed out before I went underground. Oh, the chair? My doctor says my heart is not in good shape, so I thought I'd sit with you rather than walk. The details are boring."

Pierce was sad. "You saved that for last, but it seems like it should be first. I'm sorry to hear this. I have to fly home tomorrow. I'd like to stay in contact, whatever it takes. If you have e-mail, we can use fake names if you like. I don't have to talk about cases anymore, since one topic leads to all the others anyway. Do you have people who'll care for you? Friends, a lover?"

"There's this sweet woman in Mexico, Mira, bohemian ex-pat surfer girl. She truly believes that the past, even the recent past, is not the life we're living. She's all about renewal. Plus, she's the only one besides you who knows I used to be a psychoanalyst. I left out the little part about faking my death. She just shrugged at my former career, saying she used to date a man who was once a priest, and he flipped a coin and there on the back of it was a Buddhist selling real estate. She, herself, used to be a dentist before becoming a Shaman. I don't think any one person can tell their whole life to themself, much less to another. But with her I come close. I love saying her name. Mira wants nothing to do with America. Here, I have friends for chess and music and art."

"There must be more, tell me what you can."

"As popcorn man, I tell people things about themselves. I love to invite a small awakening. Who knows where it goes? Once, I told a regular customer I was touched by the way he looks to the left when he reaches to his right hip for his wallet. I made a little game of it, except I was rather serious,

asking, 'What do you see this time Charlie? You've been looking down that road again for a sign, haven't you?' And in time,
he told me everything about his childhood that you'd tell
a therapist. And I told him things about my contradictions
that I never told my own analyst. The only complaints I get
are not enough salt or too much, or too many kernels you
could break a tooth on. Come to think of it, it's not too different than complaints you get in psychotherapy; not enough
silence or too much, or in rare cases, an idea that broke your
mind. What's a guy to do but deepen his self-awareness?"

Morissy found a pebble and threw it toward the sea, but it
only sailed ten feet. Pierce did the same. The pebbles sat side-
by-side, glistening. Morissy was in a mood.

"I gave up something unexpected when I tried for another
life. I haven't been able to gauge the distance between myself
and others. I used to worry all the time about where every-
body was in relation to me, as if I knew where *I* was the
whole time. You take that away, that un-earned comfort,
and it's a whole new ballgame. I have my tumbleweed ways.
There's a little bit of wish in us, revisionist you might say. Like
when you're on a cruise and the gentleman next to you says
he used to be a brain surgeon. But somewhere during dessert,
you take a hard look at him, the clumsy way he uses uten-
sils or lifts a glass of wine, and you wonder if he was ever a
doctor of any kind, much less a surgeon, and whether it matters now. You wonder if he's trying to romanticize himself,
since you didn't even ask what he used to do. We don't get
to know, do we?"

Pierce said that once he had a patient who spent a year in
therapy talking about his family on a beautiful ranch. Finally,
one day the fellow announced he'd made it all up, and instead
he lived in a studio apartment in a bad part of town.

"He assumed I'd kick him out of therapy immediately, but I
didn't, and a lot of things started to fit. You've got to roll with
it or you're doomed. Of course I wondered if he made up the

impoverished version too. But therapists don't go out of the office to investigate. There's one thing you can count on; if you watch people carefully, you're always finding more than you first imagined."

Morissy was transfixed watching a young girl in the sand, digging her way to China while her parents were reading books. She was feverish, almost frantic, until she dug so deep that saltwater from the ocean filled the bottom of the hole. She filled her bucket with it and it kept on coming until she finally stopped and smiled. Morissy predicted it was a pivotal moment because she smiled to herself, not to anyone else. That's how it is with discovery.

"Sometimes I imagine being a teenager again, and in my daydreams I find the boomerangs I lost in the bushes of Central Park. There was this one with my initials carved in it, made of mahogany. I hope someone interesting found it. Oh yes, Mira is good for me. She reminds me there's plenty to notice in the present. I need to be with her soon."

"I've been wondering if you're all right with our conversations these past few days. I'm still in the thick of mainstream life, practice and marriage, kids beginning to launch, meetings and vacations, everything full steam. I'm hanging on to the idea that *A* leads to *B* in some understandable way. How's that for a wishful thought? I'm glad to hear you have people who care about you. Count me among them. You'd let me know if you're in some serious trouble, right?"

Morissy, nodded, but it was a distant nod.

"I put a value on our meetings. I was getting rusty not being able to talk about this strange work of ours. What we think is happening rarely matches up with the ways people actually know us. I came to love Mexican towns and stories of everyday life, the ones that nobody goes to therapy to figure out, like where the eyes go in a tiny lie, and what our hands are saying when they touch different parts of our face during a conversation. It's been more than a little strange being a protagonist in an alternate version of myself. I can't tell you the rest. Not yet."

"Are you taking on apprentices for the popcorn business? I may try that in retirement, my own version. In therapy, nobody asks me to project myself, it just happens. Sometimes, sitting with a new person, I find myself being painted as a character in a mural that covers the whole wall. It can go the other way. Last week I was captured in the gold locket of a ninety-year-old woman. Something about a lost son."

"We do well to pay attention," mused Morissy, throwing a rock in a different direction. If he kept it up, he'd make the placements of numbers on the face of a clock.

"It's not going to be explained to us, so we can dispense with being falsely content. Better to appreciate the way we go back and forth between our internal conversations and the ones we're having with others. We talk a lot about our particular ways of being with someone, and not enough about the way someone is trying to get through to us. I have no right to say this after what I did."

Pierce picked up a piece of dried brittle seaweed that looked like the bow of a boat. He stared at it for a long time and placed it back in the sand, pointing it toward the second rock that Morissy had thrown.

Morissy saw it as an invitation. "When I arrived in Mexico, I told people I was a writer looking for the perfect setting to write a fictional novel, when really I was a fictional man who couldn't write the truth. One gentleman asked how I'd try to sort the fiction from the memories. I told him that only the tequila knows for sure. I did have thoughts of writing, but I never started the novel. Oh, I did write a bit of porn under the pseudonym *Dixie Bell LeMure*. It was rather free-ing since I explored the fantasy worlds of women hungry for sex on vacations, and made sure they were satisfied beyond their wildest dreams by young Mexican men. It was easy to project since I did my actual share of flirting with women on vacation. It's just that I was far from young. Finally, I recoiled at being anonymous. My lovers didn't speak about their lives and I didn't speak of mine. Things got blurred, and when my depression lifted, the thing I faced was the fact I could never go back to the life I nourished. In the end, all of it made me sadder. Mira, now there's a woman I needed to let into my life."

Pierce wanted to believe it all, but part of him wasn't sure. He saw what was happening; the genius in Morissy must have anticipated they were about to talk about another patient. Pierce's fifth patient was Sasha, a writer of historical fiction who had developed a special fondness for Pierce that included erotic fantasies. Pierce told how the therapy was alive with spice, although the most compelling moments were not fantasies about sleeping with Sasha. Instead, when she read sequences of her writing, he was smitten by the sex her *characters* were having. A fantasy one step removed, mixed in a polyamorous blend. When he told the tale to Morissy, all he said was, "Life is weird." Then he marked the irony by tossing three pebbles at once in the general direction of water.

Sasha's women kept dangerous secrets. The guarded parts were passed from one character to another without the author being aware. In time, Sasha read herself into her characters and it shocked the hell out of her, a kind of homecoming. Pierce was along for the ride.

"She likes my way of listening as long as I don't try to circle back to her as the author. I fight the role she seems to delegate: enchanted male who's allowed to be slow, even dumb, as long as I'm kind and don't challenge anything. Men in her stories are often used erotically. I admit, her stories are like perfume and I'm a little drawn in. Still, I'm not an automatic validator. You know how much I like understatements. I joked, pretending to be completely naive.

"I said to Sasha, 'I appreciate you didn't come to therapy for mansplaining.' It was our finest moment so far. She laughed like we were in a bar after drinking three stiff ones, and she finally told me about the real men in her life. Being polyamorous, she's used to finding combinations. She even thinking of changing her pronouns. There's an odd mix of revelation and cloaking in our meetings. She won't talk about the histories of characters in her writing, as if she's guarding their secrets from me. She keeps them tenaciously for herself, but she gets me to react. Man, I wish you could supervise me weekly."

Morissy glanced toward the horizon.

"It's a mistake to think the rocks at Moss Beach aspire to become smooth. It might be true elsewhere, but not here, and I must say, I'm a little taken with Sasha, who could have come to a lesbian therapist, a transgendered therapist, a gay male, etc., but she didn't. She doesn't want to be soothed or understood from a role you have in mind. I think you'll bring each other along without ever understanding it very much. Much of therapy is working things out in the unconscious. It's life."

Pierce spoke to the horizon, as if the seaweed was listening.

"From out there, when I swim beyond the waves in summer, I look back on the cove and think of the work it took to build the stairs leading here. They're much steeper than they seem. I think of laborers and broken tools, and the injuries that happen in construction. Should I tell Sasha what I think of the characters in her stories?"

Morissy tossed five stones to rest among Pierce's last offerings. Together they formed a constellation.

"I think not. You have foundation to build. It's best to wait for a shared image to emerge, or a new story that starts with her. Your interest in her characters is the same as your interest in her, but why say the obvious? You don't go for drinks with her after sessions, do you?"

"Hell no, our closeness is the other kind."

"Just checking," said the rock-throwing man. "Other things have been known to happen."

"Speaking of close, would you like to meet at Wood's Cove tomorrow morning. I'd love to see you once more before I fly out of here tomorrow night."

"Bring a case," said Morissy, "I'm insatiable you know."

Chapter 23

DOWN AT THE END OF DIAMOND STREET

Wood's Cove is magic, with it's magnificent entrance of twin paths converging around a succulent garden up top. There are breathless vistas from the landings. You're right around the bend from Pearl Street Beach, but it feels a world away. You can walk to a smaller cove, where pieces of sea glass wash back and forth in the shallow surge—little treasures at low tide, not always there: amber, azure, and lime, or opaque and milky white.

Morissy always had something to say at the top of stairs. It didn't matter if he was coming or going. The moment they met, he told Pierce he was planning a trip of his own, to see his sweet Mira in Mexico. Pierce wanted to believe it; the whole story of the surfer girl who became a Shaman, the small place up on Blue Bird Canyon Road, but noticed Morissy was trying to hide fatigue. He'd seen the popcorn business first hand, but doubted Morissy could sustain it much longer, if at all. Down at the end of Diamond Street, they were anxious in the quiet. Pierce was troubled, nothing new, wondering if Mexico was just a metaphor.

At first, they stayed on the larger section of beach where it's safe to enter the water and bob around for a while. Pierce took a brief swim around the rocks and returned to shore on the other side. He never ventured through the narrow channel when there was any wave action to speak of. He'd seen too many swimmers bloodied from rocks or mussels. Black razors underwater, a gamble not worth taking.

From his chair near the foot of the stairs, Morissy asked to hear another case.

"It helps the mind move on," he said, "plus if my heart is going to give out, I simply won't allow it to happen when

I'm hearing a psychotherapy tale." Pierce smiled and said he'd keep it brief, just in case they decide to make the next sailing of the Dana Pride for some whale watching. Morissy waved it off, saying he's prone enough to heaving thoughts, much less the heaving seas.

"So my sixth patient on Tuesdays is a man I'll call Bartholomew the Fourth. He's the fourth child in his family, is scheduled for 4:00 in the afternoon, and he's four minutes late by custom. When I first met him, he told me it's tough to be the fourth child. It's ok being the youngest, but other niches tend to be filled, and he has trouble defining himself. Then he says I shouldn't take him seriously when he tries to make an excuse. Ok, enough background, since we get to be sketch artists today. When he comes to sessions, he grabs some water and collapses into the chair as if the world has chased him there. He's unusual in that he recounts what happened in the last session, especially the last few minutes, as if the rest of his life is irrelevant. It's the opposite of folks who say they can't recall the previous session and expect that I'll be glad to give a synopsis."

"I'm loving it," said Morissy, taking a slug of water.

"Invariably, within minutes, Bartholomew presents a central theme that takes up the whole hour, how he's trapped in a job, in a house that's not a home, that he loves his children but he's not a particularly strong father. He's loyal and caring as a husband, but goes through the motions of life without much juice, like he's fresh out of choices when nobody makes that true except him. He's not depressed in the organic, clinical sense. He's not sure what I can do for him, and I admit that I can get caught up in the way he defeats himself, which can reduce me to an advice-giver, not my thing at all, but there I am, enacting something that's already been alienating to him. He describes a half-lived life, like his shadow side has gone missing. I find myself more curious about his wife than him, and feel badly about that."

At the use of the word *shadow*, Morissy perked up, and even stood up abruptly, to look for his own shadow. It was only a little after midday, so there wasn't much of a shadow to study. From the bluff on top, the image was that of the hands of a clock, not far apart.

"Did he mention the shadow business or was that your comment to him?"

"It was his, and no, I'm not playing Wendy to his Peter Pan."

"No worries, I check for my shadow rather often. A man also needs to make sure his treasures are safe in his pants, too. Nothing we need to analyze, of course." He winked and said, "Please continue."

"In sessions, it seems like his real effort is to get me to appreciate his delicate thinking at a distance he carefully chooses. He's boxed himself in, wonders if he's simply a dull person. I wonder along side him whether he regards dullness as a compromise solution of some kind, one that guards him from some serious, simmering anger, or maybe the experience of loss. Actually, he invites my speculation and I always feel stupid, saying things that even a brand new therapist tries to avoid. I ask him to go deeper into it, but we make a circle and become co-opted into the miasma of simplification. How many times in our careers have we heard people declare that all their problems stem from fear of intimacy, fear of being abandoned, fear of disapproval or humiliation? Worse, how many therapists say the same things, priding themselves on their acumen? Privately, I'm aware of getting upset with his way of implying his problem is mine to fix. How would you frame it back to him? I'm having a little trouble here. It's only when the water is clear that you can see what's swimming down there."

Morissy nodded as if he had known many Bartholomew's in his time, and many of them were psychotherapists.

"It's easy to get stuck in a complementary feeling, but I hope you can use it, and put it back in play. The trap here is becoming passive-aggressive. He's disappointed that life isn't more compelling, but you're disappointed he's not working very hard to make it different, so he works on refining his complaints. You find yourself dwelling in shallow theories. Your temptation is either to withdraw part of your interest or retaliate in some subtle way against his implication you haven't fixed him yet. You might get somewhere when you can see each other *through* each other, and he can say what it's like to sit with you, and what cues he's noticing. I'd want to work in the here and now, not the recap of history. It offers a chance for reciprocity. Somewhere the theme of shame rises to the surface. I don't have easy answers."

Pierce listened hard. "You know, I should mention he's got an actual sweetness. There's the suffering part he knows about and a counterpart he can't easily access. In California, in the Central Valley, sometimes you come across a child who's never seen a redwood forest or Yosemite, maybe even the ocean. You tell them what it's like, offering wonderful details. Some will shrug it off and ask if it'll be cold, or worry about mosquitos, or tell you it's enough to see a photo. Who teaches people to think like that? It's complicated, the lack of curiosity, the distrust of passion. I've always thought that one goal of therapy is to make the *not me* become a *sometimes me* experience. Anyway, by the end of the session, I have a mild headache, the kind you get when driving at night and other cars have been coming at you with headlights way too bright."

"Sometimes," Morissy said, sitting back down and crossing his legs, "it takes another person to locate a parallel theme in you. Look, it's infectious, I'm about to give some advice, and I hate doing it because it's lame. I'm tempted to suggest saying to him, 'I see you recoil sometimes and now I fear I've truly frightened you.' I think you're off to the races with him if you tell him that you can't express emotions for him by proxy, that even if you could, that part of the work belongs to him."

"It's true that life can be rather pale if you don't claim it, and it can be lonely even when you do. For sure, behaviorists are at least partly right in saying he's sustaining dullness as long as he's acting the part, but I think it's more about how he was valued coming into the world, the way people attached to him, or didn't."

"So he frightens you. I understand. Invite him into his crosscurrents, and your own. I undervalued what I used to have, and I should have been more afraid than I was. Look how I made myself vanish by kidding myself that I could evade grief. In all this talk, I wonder if Bart has seen something horrible, something terribly aggressive, or he couldn't stop his parents from fighting even when he put himself in the middle? Blame and shame; there's a pair to draw to. I think his way of remembering the details of sessions is a plea for you to remember him, also a bit of a demand. We therapists are relentless, always wondering about what's been experienced but disavowed. Who knows? Probably we're both off the mark and the main story is he's much more gentle than his father wanted him to be. Now the son feels deficient, now he reminds his therapist what happened, again and again, but leaves out the source of emotions. Look how easily Bart he gets us to speculate. Interesting man, but we'll have to leave it for now, my friend."

Pierce realized that Morissy might have been talking about himself, just a bit, or at least something universal. Pierce recalled that Morissy's own parents died violently. Once, during a walk among falling leaves, Morissy told him that every time he was honored for an achievement or lectured in front of a crowd, he kept hoping to see the faces of his parents in the audience. He would even come close to an orchestra pit sometimes, right to the edge of the stage, until it became a trademark of sorts.

Chapter 24

SEA GLASS AT LOVER'S COVE

They rose from the sand and walked a few steps to the tiny Lover's Cove. Pierce carried the chair and Morissy carried the doubt. They stood in the water after raising their pants to the knees. The tide and season were right, and each was rewarded by a piece of sea glass tumbling at their feet. Everything was in motion, water coming and going, with large round pebbles crashing painfully against their ankles. The bitter comes in with the sweet. Each put their prize in a pocket and stepped back to the dry coarse sand.

Back in NYC, when they were first becoming friends, Morissy told Pierce that when he walked into his home after the tragedy of his parent's deaths, he just stood there, studying the furniture for the longest time. How could the furniture stay when his parents weren't there? How could anything be allowed to be there? Pierce had the image in mind when he asked Morissy a final question.

"How do you know when someone is speaking to you without filters?" Morissy took a moment to be with his delicate muse.

"It's when the eyes match the words and the words go slow around the curves. The eyes look for an anchor, and it's likely to be something other than you, so you shouldn't assume the person is evading you just because they're not looking at you. It feels like they're speaking internally at the same time they're speaking to you, and you're both transported. You sense it more in the spine than the mind. I can't explain it otherwise. I don't think people get better in therapy because of the conscious actions of the therapist, but in the floundering effort of intention and empathy and determined curiosity; it's a brew of molten metals. I liken it to a cast, a sculpture that starts to form. If it doesn't feel right, you can always melt it down. It's still not right. Another rises, and something unexpected makes it feel more honest. It begins to surprise you—the goodness of fit. Stand back; see if it holds. Don't worry about the shape it's taking. That's all I've got for you, my friend."

Pierce took a moment to touch his friend's shoulder, knowing it was time to part.

"When my time comes, I'd like my ashes in the sea, within view of Three Arch Bay, a place of astonishing beauty where I was a lifeguard during college. People came to the beach in a simple way, with only a folding chair, a small umbrella, water and a book. The beach is private, or I would have taken you there. People living there don't take it for granted. At Three Arch Bay, parents weren't cruel to their children when it was time to leave. I saw too many kids at other beaches being dragged by the arm from their sand castles. At Three Arch Bay, the dusk is as welcome as the dawn."

Morissy said he'd like to be interred on a mountainside in Mexico, overlooking a little valley with a seasonal river. He'd visited such a place, where arbors hold climbing roses to the sun and beautiful red rocks keep their heat for half the night. The bells of a church in town can be heard along the path to the cemetery.

Chapter 25

RETURN OF THE CLOCK

At the top of the stairs, Morissy paused to mention their visit in the hospital years ago. "It's about time you presented more of that case you started when I was laid up after my prostate surgery. I knew it would be a good one. I remember something about Virginia Woolf before I fell off. I had the thought you might ask your patient more about the book. I recall you saying the man suffered from the delusion he was the clock that nibbled at the June day."

Pierce was astounded, remembering that Morissy was fast asleep, or at least in a morphine haze.

"Are you freaking kidding me? Of course I recall the visit. I was trying to keep my promise, to always present you a case as long as you're willing. I invented a doozy of a case, but I only got a few sentences into it since I was making it up as I went along. Fault me, but I wasn't going to burden you with one of my real patients. I just wasn't going to do it. So, in a way, because you're still alive, I'd like a little credit!"

"But you didn't invent anything," said Morissy, looking over the top of his glasses. "There may be something I'm missing, but surely you were talking about yourself. I think it was a spontaneous association to living with all the things that shred your understanding, your sense of control and proportion, all the problems we face when something shakes us up. You probably can't remember this, but you had a premonition that I was sick before I knew. The clock must have represented dread, the inevitable parceling of experience. It's the oldest burden of all."

"But I was so sure you were asleep. You were brilliantly funny during that visit, refusing to talk about yourself, fighting fear with your sense of humor. Besides, at the end of that epic sentence about by Virginia Woolf, the clock simply told the correct time to two gentlemen. I was just goofing with you."

In similar moments in the old days, Morissy was famous for slipping into his imitation of a British scholar from Oxford University, musing, penetrating the air. He did it again.

"Yes, quite, hmmm, or so you thought. Not so simple. You happened to visit me at 1:30 that afternoon, the same as the clock on Harley Street in the novel. Coincidence? I think not. Perhaps we can meet again and you can delve further into this case. It was terribly limited, you know, a tease really. Something about your fictional patient having a delusion. There's more to it, you know."

With that, they parted with a hand on each other's shoulder. Pierce stood at the place of parting while his friend walked down the road toward an old pickup truck loaded to the gills with a green tarp over the contents. Morissy was on the move.

Chapter 26

NOEMI

Pierce took an extra moment to find his keys. The walk to his car was solemn. Main Beach at sunset became his goal, to the spot where he first saw the pelicans. He'd seen dozens of other pelicans in the last few days, but none were etched in memory like the original six. On the Pacific Coast Highway, he was nearly killed by a speeding van that went far out of its lane. Someone was desperate to get somewhere, weaving in and out of traffic. It clipped the mirror off his car; the man didn't even look back. At least the mirror was fixable. He hoped Morissy had more time, that he'd have a chance to see him again. Everything around him was a call to alertness. When he pulled over to collect himself, a text from his wife Clair came in. No words were attached. It was a photo of purple clouds at sunrise from a beach in Costa Rica. He sent back a photo of Wood's Cove that he'd just taken. It was a complete language.

By then it was dusk at Main Beach. There was a two-foot swell at low tide, a fact that locals would know just by the sound of waves and their intervals, even if they didn't look at the sea. A child knows the mood of the mother in a similar way, even when she's out of sight. It comes in the pattern of breathing, the sound of turning a page when she's reading.

In the fall of night he headed inland using his best merging skills on the freeway. You have to get up to speed and mean it; then the world makes room for you. It's dangerous to lack confidence while merging, at least in Southern California.

He drove past two men who'd been in an accident, probably tailgating at 80 mph, and had gotten out of their cars to face off, right on the edge of the freeway. One man broke the window of the other's car with a tire iron. The other man seemed to be reaching for something in his glove box, probably a gun. Typical California moment. Everyone was staring. Traffic backed up quickly. Several drivers got on cell phones. The world was 911.

While stopped on the freeway, Pierce's cell phone rang; it was his practice partner René. She was excited and glad to hear his voice.

"Hatley, you won't believe this but your mystery caller left a message. It's not one of your patients at all! We had all this speculation, all this doubt. It's a woman called Noemi, apologizing for hanging up so many times. She's in the Philippines, does telemarketing, making five hundred calls a day, but her question was to ask if you're really a psychologist and can you help? Your outgoing message says only that you're Dr. Pierce, and she managed to Google you, found your photo and practice description, but has no money. Her son was just killed by the government for suspicion of using drugs. He wasn't even a dealer. They came and shot him in the street. Her local doctor is no help. She says she's falling apart, that her marriage is no good, she hates her job and can't go back to work at the fish market. The poor gal was crying. Of course I left the message so you can hear it yourself."

"My God, of course I'll call her. Maybe I can only offer kindness and a little hope. Noemi you say. Thank you René, extra bottle of wine for you for looking after my practice. I thought I needed a few days away from serious thinking. You won't believe what happened instead."

"Oh, Hatley, that's not all. Your patient Ava also called, says she needs to see you as soon as you get back, that she's been having dreams of her old therapist, the fellow who died, and they're starting to have conversations in her dreams. It's freakishly real to her. I miss our talks and I have some really puzzling cases of my own to talk about. I'm stuck in a few and haven't mentioned it. We need to find more time. One more thing; someone sent you a letter with no return address, beautiful,

like calligraphy from another century. It looked very feminine, very personal. The thing has very strong energy. I put it
on your desk."

Pierce let go of the steering wheel and covered his eyes,
trying to bring up the image of the distant Noemi, crying
into the phone. *I wish I could tell all this to Morissy,* he thought,
imagining himself back home in the act of putting his piece
of sea glass on the top of his dresser in a shallow mahogany
bowl. He asked René when the call came in. She said, "Just
now, I'll give you the number."

She did, and he called, and a woman named Noemi was
on the other end, like she was sitting next to him in the car.
It was unbelievable—the ease of voice, the rush of words, the
poverty of what he could offer in her time of horrible grief.
Still, he tried to ground her. There was a sister she hadn't seen
for years, a grudge to settle, a place in a church she knows, a
letter she needed to write to the son she just lost.

The last view of Pierce was an aerial one, like birds might
see, of a man stuck on the freeway, with people around him
honking. You could hear the approach of sirens. Nobody was
going anywhere. Pierce reclined his seat at far as it would go.

He leaned back, closed his eyes. A ripple of warm air chased
him from the sun's last moments. He summoned his recent
image from the beach; sixty gulls or more were heading north
toward the Back Bay at Newport, where they settle for the
night, protected on little islands. The pelicans were heading
south. Not a single cloud was present in the evening sky, but
he knew that rain was coming.

•

About the Author

J.L. COOPER was an author and psychologist in Sacramento, California. His writing highlights the lyricism in everyday life, relational mysteries, and the elevation of subjective experience. He has received five literary awards in fiction, nonfiction, poetry, and essay, including the *Tupelo Quarterly Prose Open Prize*, TQ9, judged by Pulitzer winner Adam Johnson, and the Grand Prize in Poetry, *Crosswinds Poetry Journal*, 2018, judged by Pulitzer winner in criticism Lloyd Schwartz. His full-length book of poetry, *An Ocean Large Enough* (David Robert Books) is available on Amazon Books, as are his two books of short stories, *The Sages of 47th Street* and *A Perfect Stillness*, and a novella, *Spell of the Pelicans*. His short stories, poetry and a craft piece have appeared or are forthcoming in numerous journals including *The Manhattan Review, The Comstock Review, New Millennium Writings, Oberon Poetry Magazine, Story Quarterly, Cutthroat, Hippocampus, Leveler, The Tishman Review, 3 Elements Review, Structo,* and several other journals and anthologies. His website is: jlcooper.net.

James passed away at home with his family in October, 2018 after a 5-year battle with cancer.

Also by J.L. Cooper

Available through Amazon, Barnes & Noble,
Book Depository, and most online book retailers.

PO Box #3092
Citrus Heights, CA 95611-3092
fivewarblers.wordpress.com